Sherlock Holmes and the Curse of Neb-Heka-Ra

By

Margaret Walsh

Paperback ISBN 978-1-80424-102-8
Epub ISBN 978-1-80424-103-5
PDF ISBN 978-1-80424-104-2

Published by MX Publishing
335 Princess Park Manor, Royal Drive,
London, N11 3GX
www.mxpublishing.co.uk

Cover design by Brian Belanger

For my cousins Janelle & Shauna.
Your support means a lot to me.

Chapter 1

The newspapers are full of the amazing discoveries that Howard Carter has made in Egypt. The discovery of the tomb of an unknown boy-king: Tutankhamun and his untold riches. Sitting in the sun reading the stories, my mind went back to an extraordinary case that my dear friend, Mr. Sherlock Holmes, handled in the last decades of the last century.

I never wrote about it at the time. Indeed, I felt the very strangeness of the case would repel people. However, since other, equally strange, and gruesome, cases have been well-received upon their recent publication, I am once again endeavouring to relate the tale in a way that does justice to my friend's formidable intellect.

It was a warm autumn morning when a messenger from Inspector Giles Lestrade arrived at 221B Baker Street, where I was once again in residence.

The young police constable almost saluted Holmes in his eagerness. "Mr. Holmes, Inspector Lestrade sends his regards and asks if you would come at once." The young man paused for breath before blurting out, "There's been a murder, sir. A real rum one at that!"

Holmes arched an eyebrow in slight amusement. "Indeed." He turned to me. "Care to join me, Watson?"

"Naturally, Holmes, if Lestrade will not mind." I looked at the police constable with an expression of polite enquiry on my face.

The constable nodded. "Of course, Dr. Watson. The inspector just said Mr. Holmes because he didn't know if you would be here."

"Then I will come."

"Excellent," Holmes said, rubbing his hands together briskly.

We donned our hats and coats and followed the constable down to where a police brougham waited by the curb. The constable scrambled up to sit beside the driver as Holmes and I entered the vehicle. The driver chucked the reins, and we clopped gently away down Baker Street.

The ride was a short one: the destination proving to be a genteel and elegant townhouse in Wimpole Mews in Marylebone. Wimpole Mews was a quiet little street close by Harley Street.

Our destination was obvious as two uniformed police officers stood sentry outside the open door of the townhouse in question. Our escort showed us into the building then scurried back outside to join his colleagues.

We could hear Lestrade's voice coming from a nearby room, so we hastened to join him.

Upon hearing our footsteps in the hall, Lestrade came out to join us. Our Scotland Yard friend was looking harassed and unhappy. His moustache drooping in a way that telegraphed his misery.

The cause of his unhappiness became obvious when a

younger man, obviously a doctor going by the Gladstone bag that he clutched to his chest in a manner reminiscent of a child with a toy, came out of the room behind him. This man, whose sickly pallor made me wonder if he were going to faint, scuttled past us and out of the door.

Lestrade watched him go and sighed deeply, running a hand across his face in agitation.

Holmes watched the scurrying man disappear into the street. "Who was that?"

"A local doctor," Lestrade replied sourly. "The police surgeon for D Division has taken his family and gone to Margate for a month. That useless young man is filling in for him. More at home with coughs than corpses, I am afraid. I am sending the body to A Division for the post-mortem." Lestrade pulled a face. "Dr. Bond is not going to thank me for adding to his workload."

"May we see the corpse? You did ask for our assistance after all," said Holmes.

Lestrade nodded and gestured to the doorway he had come out of. "In there, gentlemen."

Holmes and I walked to the door and then stopped in surprise.

The room was obviously a study of some kind. A heavy oaken desk sat near the window to take advantage of the meagre sunlight. Green velvet curtains framed the window. Mahogany bookcases lined three walls. From what I could see from where

I stood, the books on the shelves were mostly texts on general medicine and surgery. Something appeared to be missing from the room, but I could not think what it could be.

My eyes were drawn to the area behind the desk where a form could be seen stretched out on the floor.

"Dr. Horace Simpson," Lestrade said, indicating the body on the floor. "Surgeon by profession. Mostly taught at St. Bartholomew's Hospital these days. He did, however, have a consulting room on Harley Street."

Holmes had moved towards the body as Lestrade was talking. I joined him.

The late Dr. Horace Simpson had been tied up. He lay on his back with his hands and ankles bound tightly together in a manner that Americans describe as "hog-tied."

The truly alarming thing was the fact that his head was completely covered with sand. Not even a whisker could be seen protruding.

"That is certainly different," Holmes observed.

"That is the reason I sent for you, Holmes," Lestrade replied. "It is clearly a case of murder, and it is equally clear that I am going to need your assistance with this. Why kill someone with sand?"

"He may not have been killed with sand," I said. "It may have been placed there afterwards."

"A good point, Watson," said Holmes. "The post-mortem will tell us the exact manner of death. Whichever it proves to be, the sand is clearly important."

"How can you know this?" I asked.

"Someone went to a great deal of effort to bring the sand here. Clean, fine, sand is not easily accessible in this part of London. If all the killer wanted to do was bury the man's head, then mud from the Thames or dirt from a garden would have served just as well. No, Watson, the sand is most definitely important. But as to its exact importance, I cannot yet say."

Holmes looked at Lestrade. "You can take the corpse away now. I should like to attend the post-mortem, however."

Lestrade nodded and then went to the door to fetch a couple of constables. They came in carrying a stretcher and a length of canvas. The body of the unfortunate Dr. Simpson was wrapped up and carried out leaving only a mess of sand upon the floor.

"Who found the body?" Holmes asked.

"Simpson's secretary, Nigel Withers," Lestrade replied. "I asked him to wait in the kitchen, along with Simpson's two assistants who both live here as well."

"Household staff?" Holmes asked.

"None that live on the premises. A cook and a cleaning lady come in daily. This is a bachelor establishment."

I looked around and realized why I had thought there was something missing from the room. There were no feminine touches to the room at all. No vases of fresh cut flowers. No dried flowers preserved under glass domes. The room was purely masculine.

"Time to have a word with Mr. Withers," Holmes said. "Is there a suitable room available, Lestrade?"

The inspector nodded. "I thought we might use the library on the first floor."

"Lead the way, Lestrade, and send one of your constables to fetch Mr. Withers."

We followed Lestrade out of the room, paused as he spoke briefly to one of the constables at the door, and then followed him up the stairs to a room that appeared to be directly above the study below and of very similar dimensions and appearance. Except that the desk had been replaced with a comfortable armchair. A small table sat nearby with a bottle of brandy, a couple of glasses, and a gasogene for producing soda water to go with the brandy. Several chairs, obviously from the kitchen, had been set out in a semi-circle in front of the armchair. Holmes waved Lestrade to the comfortable chair and began to prowl the shelves. I took one of the chairs from the group and dragged it over to sit next to Lestrade.

Footsteps could be heard on the stairs. The door opened and a tall, young, man, with mouse-brown hair, watery blue eyes that blinked at us from behind a pair of tortoiseshell spectacles, and a somewhat bewildered air, entered the room.

He sat in one of the chairs and looked at us.

"You are Nigel Withers?" Lestrade asked.

The young man blinked. "Yes. I told you that earlier."

"Yes, you did, but I was not interviewing you at the time, so I needs must ask again."

"My apologies, Inspector Lestrade, I have no idea how any of this works."

"Understood, Mr. Withers. Now, can you tell us what happened?

Nigel Withers looked at me, then at Holmes, who had come to stand behind Lestrade. "Excuse me, Inspector, but before we begin, who are these gentlemen?"

"This is Mr. Sherlock Holmes and his associate, Dr. John Watson. Given the strange circumstances of the death, it was thought prudent to involve them from the beginning."

Withers nodded slowly. "Yes, that makes sense. This whole thing is very strange indeed. I cannot imagine who would want to kill Dr. Simpson. He had no enemies. If one even has enemies these days." He blinked at us owlishly. "I hardly know where to start."

"At the beginning, Mr. Withers, if you please," said Lestrade. "With your full name and address."

"I am Nigel Bruce Withers. I reside here in this house in Wimpole Mews. Or I did. I have no idea where I will go now."

"I understand that you found Dr. Simpson?" Holmes asked.

"I did. When I came downstairs for breakfast, I noticed that the door to the study was ajar. This was unusual as Dr. Simpson was quite set on doors being kept closed. When I went to close it, I spotted sand on the floor just inside the door. I could think of no reason why there should be sand on the floor, so I went into the study." Withers paused, his face paling further. "You know what I found. It was ghastly. Simply ghastly."

I rose from my seat and poured a measure of Simpson's brandy into a glass and handed it to Withers. "Drink this."

The man made as if to protest. "Doctor's orders," I said firmly. "You have had a nasty shock."

He nodded mutely but took the glass from me and sipped slowly at the brandy.

"I understand that you were Dr. Simpson's secretary," Holmes said.

Withers nodded. "Yes. I kept his appointment book for him, handled his correspondence, and his accounts. That sort of thing."

"Did Dr. Simpson have any appointments last night?" asked Lestrade.

Withers shook his head. "No. He was to be instructing at Barts today. He never went out of an evening before he lectured. We had dinner and he sent me to bed saying he would lock up himself."

"Was that his usual practice?" Holmes asked.

Withers frowned and lowered the glass. "No. It wasn't," he said slowly. "I usually did the locking up of the house. The doctor preferred not to be bothered with household matters."

"Could he have been expecting a visitor that he did not want you to know about?" Holmes asked.

Withers started to disagree, then stopped. "It is possible," he said thoughtfully. "My bedroom is at the back of the house. I cannot hear when anyone comes to the front door. Cartwright and Evans would not have heard either. Their rooms are right at the top of the house."

"We will need to see Dr. Simpson's appointment book," Lestrade said.

Withers got to his feet. "I shall fetch it for you."

"Thank you, Mr. Withers. And if you could tell Mr. Cartwright and Mr. Evans that we would like to see them."

"Separately or together?"

"Separately, if you please."

Withers nodded and ducked out of the room. He was back within minutes with a frown on his face. "I cannot find Dr. Simpson's appointment book. It is not in my office. It must have been left in his office at Barts. Do you wish me to go to Barts and fetch it?"

Holmes raised an eyebrow. "Is it usual for the appointment book not to be in your office?"

"Oh yes. Dr. Simpson always took it with him to make note of appointments he set up whilst there. He often forgot to bring it home, however, so I usually had to make a trip to Barts the next day to retrieve it."

"If you could bring the appointment book to Baker Street within the next few days, I would be grateful," Holmes said.

Withers nodded and left the room.

"Next few days?" Lestrade asked. "Why not today?"

"I think it is highly unlikely that Dr. Simpson's murderer made an appointment with him. His behaviour last night tends to indicate a meeting of a more clandestine nature than one would find scheduled in an appointment book," Holmes replied.

Lestrade nodded his agreement and settled back in his chair to await the next man.

Robert Cartwright, when he arrived, proved to be a brawny young man with a forthright expression in his sharp blue eyes.

"I'm Robert Cartwright. Mr. Withers said you wanted to speak with me."

"That is correct. Please take a seat, Mr. Cartwright," Lestrade said, gesturing to the array of chairs in front of us.

Cartwright lowered himself into one of the chairs and looked at us. "I'm not sure I can tell you gentlemen anything. I heard nothing last night. Didn't know what had happened until Mr. Withers came crashing into the kitchen white as a sheet. Me and Caleb got him set down and then went to look for ourselves." The man shook his head slowly. "It's a rum do and no mistake."

"Caleb?" I asked.

"Caleb Evans," Cartwright replied. "Dr. Simpson's other assistant."

"What happened after you and Mr. Evans saw Dr. Simpson on the floor?" Lestrade asked.

"I sent Caleb to fetch the police, shut the study door and went back to the kitchen to make sure Mr. Withers was all right. He's a surgeon's secretary, but he doesn't deal with the sharp end, so to speak."

"What do you mean?" Lestrade asked.

"He does the book work and such. Caleb and me, we did the dirty work."

"Dirty work?" Lestrade asked.

"Clean up the mess after surgeries mostly. Dr. Simpson operated on private cases at Barts. He rented an operating theatre from them when he needed it. We cleaned up after he was done. Dr. Simpson also did small surgeries at people's homes. Removing tonsils and such. We carried his equipment and cleaned up." Cartwright gave us a quick, tight, grin. "Those sort of surgeries are done in the kitchen. Cooks get a bit cranky if you leave even a spot of blood on the table."

Lestrade shot me an inquiring look. I nodded. Kitchen surgery was not uncommon, but it always struck me as borderline barbaric and not particularly hygienic.

"Thank you, Mr. Cartwright. That will be all. Would you please ask Mr. Evans to join us?" Lestrade said.

Cartwright got to his feet, nodded, and slipped out of the door.

Caleb Evans, when he arrived, appeared to have little in common with Robert Cartwright but size. He was a brawny man, dull of eye, and somewhat surly of character.

Evans took the seat indicated and glared at us sullenly. "I don't know what you think I can tell you. I never properly saw Dr. Simpson's body this morning. I was behind Bob when we went into study. Bob took one look and sent me for the rozzers."

"Did you hear anything at all last night?" Lestrade asked.

Evans shook his head. "Nothing odd, anyway. The rats were busy in the attic as always. Me and Bob went to our beds at our usual time…"

"Which is?" Lestrade asked, making a note in his notebook.

"About 8 o'clock. Today was a surgery day. So we needed to be up early. Heard Mr. Withers moving about in his room about half an hour later. Nothing after that."

"And this morning?"

"Got up at 6 o'clock. Had a quick wash and went down with Bob to the kitchen. The cook comes in to make luncheon, and dinner, and she leaves stuff for breakfast. This morning it was cold kedgeree and some devilled kidneys to be reheated. I got busy with that, Bob was getting out the plates and cutlery,

15

when Mr. Withers came running into the kitchen, all shook up. Started babbling on about Dr. Simpson being dead. So, we went to have a look, and then Bob sent me for the rozzers, as I said before."

Lestrade finished his notes, then looked at Evans and nodded. "Thank you, Mr. Evans, that will be all."

The man got to his feet and walked to the door. He paused and turned back to us. "What do we do now? Me and Bob, and Mr. Withers as well, we haven't got a place to go to."

"I am sure there will not be a problem with you remaining here for a short time while you seek another position. Dr. Simpson's beneficiaries may have other ideas, of course. But for the moment I believe it best if you remain here," said Holmes.

Evans nodded and left the room.

Lestrade looked at Holmes. "Leave them where we can find them if we need them, eh?"

"Indeed," replied Holmes.

Lestrade closed his notebook, placed it and his pen in his pocket, and then got to his feet.

"Well gentlemen, I think it's time we left, don't you? We do have a post-mortem to attend, after all."

Chapter Two

We did not have to travel far – only to the Westminster Hospital. There can be very few hospitals with such a picturesque location as the Westminster. It sat on the Broad Sanctuary opposite Westminster Abbey. From some of the windows a pleasant view of the Thames and the Houses of Parliament were to be had. However, the morgue at the Westminster Hospital smelled as all morgues do; the iron tang of blood overlaid with the acrid stench of raw carbolic.

A Division's police surgeon, Dr. Thomas Bond, had barely begun the post-mortem when we arrived.

Bond, with whom we had had several dealings in the past, greeted me as a colleague, and Holmes and Lestrade with his usual cordial demeanour.

"Inspector Lestrade," Bond said, "You do send me the most interesting corpses. More so than any other detective."

"I seem to be given the more interesting cases these days," Lestrade replied. "Have you found anything, Doctor?"

Bond gestured for us to join him at the table. "As I said, interesting corpse. One of your constables told me it was murder?"

"It almost has to be," Lestrade replied. "The man was found with his head buried in sand."

"You forgot to mention that he was tied up like a beast for slaughter, Lestrade," Holmes added drily.

Bond ignored the byplay. "I have swabbed the mouth,

nose and throat. There was a great deal of sand in all three." He gestured to his assistant, who came over and rolled the body into its side. "As you can see by the lividity, Dr. Simpson had been dead for some time before he was found. The blood has pooled in the tissues of his back. The amount suggests to me that the man was dead some six to eight hours before he was found."

Lestrade retrieved his notebook and pen from his pocket and began to take notes.

The assistant gently lowered the body back down and Bond picked up a scalpel. He pointed it at the victim's wrists and ankles. "As Mr. Holmes noted, the victim was restrained. I have also examined the back of the victim's head. There is no sign of blunt force trauma. Whatever the method was that he was induced to be restrained, it did not involve any blows to the head. Nor could were there any signs of burned skin around the nose and mouth, which rules out the use of chloroform." Bond looked back down at the corpse. "The victim, though approaching middle-age, was relatively fit. It seems to me to be unlikely that one person was able to overpower him."

Holmes, Lestrade, and I stepped back to allow Dr. Bond and his assistant to work freely. The chest was sliced open, and the ribs broken with the gentle economy of movement that showed that Bond did this task every day. The lungs were removed and opened. Bond hummed to himself.

Holmes stepped closer. "What have you found?"

"Sand in the lungs. Not a large amount, but some. I suspect I will also find sand in the digestive tract. I do not even have to look at the eyes for petechial haemorrhaging to give cause of death."

"For the records, please, Dr. Bond," said Lestrade.

"A full report will be sent to Scotland Yard later today, but for now it is sufficient to say that the cause of death was asphyxiation with sand, by person or persons unknown." Bond looked at Lestrade. "It is most definitely a case of murder."

We left the Westminster Hospital and accompanied Lestrade back to his office at Scotland Yard. Lestrade was already sinking into a gloomy mood. "This is going to be a bad one. A respectable man killed, a strange method of murder, no motive, and no suspects!"

Holmes shook his head. "There is a motive, Lestrade. There is always a motive. We may not understand what that motive is at this precise moment, but no one kills without one, no matter how absurd that motive may appear to the rational mind."

"You think the killer is insane?" Lestrade stared at Holmes.

Holmes shot him an irritable look. "I did not say that. A lack of immediate understanding on our part does not equate to insanity in the murderer." He paused. "Or rather, murderers. I agree with Dr. Bond's conclusions. There is more than one person involved in this crime. As to suspects..." He paused. "I admit that we have none at the moment."

"Withers is going to retrieve Simpson's appointment

book," I said. "Perhaps there will be someone in there."

Lestrade sighed. "At the very least we will have to speak with them. For elimination purposes if nothing else."

"Indeed," said Holmes.

I expected that we would receive the appointment book before anything else occurred, but in this instance, I was very wrong.

A constable was on our doorstep just after sunrise the next morning.

"Inspector Lestrade requests your presence, gentlemen. I have a brougham waiting for you."

I exchanged a look with Holmes. It was clear that he was not expecting the summons either. We donned our hats and coats and accompanied the constable downstairs.

The brougham took us towards the river. It was clear that we were heading towards Westminster. At that time of the morning there was little private transport on the roads, but delivery carts still hampered our progress somewhat.

The brougham stopped near Westminster Bridge and the constable led us down to a small area below the bridge, hard by the Houses of Parliament, and the glorious gothic Clock Tower, designed by Augustus Pugin, that housed the magnificent bell clock known as Big Ben. Though that name strictly belonged only to the largest of the clock's five bells. The tower was an awe-inspiring reminder of the greatness of the British Empire.

Lestrade was waiting for us, a beaming smile on his

face. "It is solved!" he announced.

Holmes raised an eyebrow.

"Surely you do not mean Dr. Simpson's murder?" I asked.

"I do indeed, Doctor Watson." Lestrade waved a hand towards the river. "The body of Robert Cartwright was dragged from the river little more than an hour ago. Clearly the man killed his employer, and in a fit of remorse, killed himself. Mystery solved."

Holmes snorted and went to look at the body for himself.

I was searching my mind for something to say, when Holmes straightened up from his close, but swift, examination of the corpse and turned to Lestrade.

Holmes's expression was inscrutable, but his tone when he spoke, was scathing. "Suicide? Then pray, Lestrade, kindly explain the obvious rope abrasions on Cartwright's wrists and ankles."

"What?" Lestrade looked aghast. He hurried to my friend's side, bending to examine the corpse closely. Straightening up, he let out a groan.

"Really, Lestrade," my friend said, "that sort of sloppy jumping to conclusions is something I expect from Athelney Jones. It is clear from the marks that Cartwright was tied up in the same manner as Simpson before his body was disposed of in the Thames."

"Was the man even drowned?" I asked.

"Impossible to tell," Holmes replied. "I trust that the good Dr. Bond will be able to answer that question during the post-mortem."

Lestrade hung his head and scuffed his feet against the ground. I was irresistibly reminded of a small boy being scolded for scrumping fruit. He turned to stare out at the river for a few moments, obviously trying to contain his embarrassment. Lestrade took a deep breath, then turned and signalled to the accompanying constables to place the corpse of the unfortunate Cartwright onto a stretcher.

We followed quietly behind as the constables carried their burden on the short journey to the Westminster Hospital.

Dr. Bond and his assistant were waiting for us, silently transferring the corpse to a rough wooden surgical table. Those tables always unsettled me. Deep grooves along the sides allowed blood and other bodily fluids to drain into buckets placed on the floor at each corner. The wood itself was darkly stained with old blood.

Bond's assistant divested Cartwright of his sodden garments, chucking them in a heap in the corner. Holmes made a clucking noise with his tongue; his annoyance clear at the mishandling of what could be evidence. He sorted through the wet mess as Bond began to work.

I kept one eye on Dr. Bond and the other on my friend's perambulations around the morgue. Holmes found some rope sitting upon a table in the corner which he began to examine. Finally, he brought it across to us.

"Was this the rope that bound Dr. Simpson?" he asked.

Bond looked up briefly and nodded. "It is indeed. I left it there. I thought Scotland Yard may want it as evidence."

Lestrade looked blankly at Holmes. "It's rope. Available anywhere."

"There are many different sorts of rope, Lestrade," my friend chided the inspector. "There are tarred ropes for use on sailing ships, for example. This appears to be a much finer rope. I would suggest it comes from a child's skipping rope, or possibly rope kept for household use. It is lightweight and reasonably smooth, with a distinctive twill. It is clearly not cheap rope." He paused. "I really should write a monograph upon the subject. It could prove to be of great use in the science of detection."

"Holmes..." Lestrade began.

I was beginning to feel a little sorry for Lestrade. He was having an exceedingly trying morning.

Holmes stepped up to the table and lifted the arm of the corpse. He lined a piece of the rope against the wrist. The rope aligned with the harsh red burns upon the skin. "As you can see, the abrasions on Cartwright's wrist were made by an identical piece of rope. No doubt cut from the same ball."

"Good Lord!" I exclaimed.

Holmes carefully cut a piece from the rope and tucked it away in his pocket.

Bond looked across the table at my friend. "That is very

interesting, Mr. Holmes. And I shall now tell you something interesting."

"What would that be, Dr. Bond?" Holmes asked.

"This man did not die in the Thames."

"He wasn't drowned?" Lestrade asked.

"Oh, he drowned, all right," Bond replied. "But not in the Thames. There is no Thames water in his lungs. The river is horribly polluted as you well know."

Dr. Bond was correct. The river had been cleaned up after the Great Stink of 1858 in which the summer heat had caused the stench of human waste and industrial effluent that was daily discharged into the Thames to build up to such a state that Parliament could not sit for the smell penetrated the inner recesses of the building. Joseph Bazalgette's sewer system had lessened the flow of contaminants into the river but had not stopped it. Anyone falling into the river, if they did not drown, was still likely to contract cholera or typhoid fever or both.

Bond continued, "There is water in this man's lungs, but it is clean. There is no sign of Thames mud, nor effluent of any sort, in his respiratory system. I can only conclude that he was drowned elsewhere, and his body placed in the Thames."

"For us to find," Lestrade said gloomily.

"Yes," said Dr. Bond. He gave Lestrade a dark look. "It looks like you have a madman on your hands, Inspector. God help you all."

Chapter Three

We left Westminster Hospital in a sombre mood. Lestrade returned to Scotland Yard, and Holmes and I to Baker Street.

We had not long returned when Mrs. Hudson tapped on our door to announce a visitor. She escorted Mr. Nigel Withers into the room. The man was clutching a large, leather-bound, book to his chest.

He handed the tome to Holmes. "That is Dr. Simpson's appointment book, Mr. Holmes."

Holmes laid the book on the desk and flicked through it briefly. I stood and watched over his shoulder as he did so. It was a typical doctor's appointment book. Days and times were laid out neatly in a fine copperplate hand, with a few other entries in an almost cryptic scrawl that was probably done by Simpson himself.

Holmes paused at one entry from about two weeks earlier. I understood what caught his attention. Eight o'clock of an evening was an odd time to be operating.

Holmes called Withers' attention to the page. The man came over and looked at the entry.

"Ah yes. Dr. Simpson was very economical. He used one appointment book for both professional and personal appointments. The evening ones are almost always personal. That one was at Mr. Robert Wilson's home. The man is a banker in the City. The week before that was a function at Lord

Reginald Ashmoore's town house."

Holmes's eyebrows rose. "Dr. Simpson kept interesting company."

Withers shrugged. "Dr. Simpson was a convivial man, Mr. Holmes. People liked his company. He was a popular guest at dinner parties."

Holmes nodded and closed the appointment book. "I shall go over this at my leisure, if I may?"

Withers nodded. "Of course, Mr. Holmes. Dr. Simpson has no use for it now."

"Indeed."

"Mr. Withers," I said, "Are you aware of this morning's tragic discovery?"

"The death of Robert Cartwright?"

"Yes."

"A constable came and advised us this morning." He shook his head. "I am leaving today. That place is cursed. If you gentlemen need to find me, I shall be back residing with my elderly mother in Pimlico. I gave the address to the constable this morning. I have urged Evans to move out as well. He will not. I fear he has nowhere else to go."

Withers turned and walked to the door. He paused in the doorway and looked back at us. "There is one odd thing, though I cannot see how it could be related to these murders."

"What is that Mr. Withers?" asked Holmes.

"I did an inventory of Dr. Simpson's bag. A new, and rather expensive, bone saw is missing."

"Could he simply have mislaid it?" I asked.

Withers shook his head. "Dr. Simpson was very particular about his instruments. He would not even lend them to colleagues." With that he left the room, closing the door behind him.

"What do you make of it, Holmes?" I asked.

"Make of what?"

"The mystery of the missing bone-saw?"

Holmes snorted. "I find myself in agreement with you, Watson. The bone-saw was most likely mislaid. It is certainly an unlikely object to steal, except possibly by an impecunious medical student."

I chuckled. "The good Lord knows there are enough of them. I used to be one." I paused for a moment. "Holmes, what do we do now?"

"I do believe, my dear Watson, that it is time to have a brief chat with Simpson's Wimpole Mews neighbours."

The weather was pleasant, so we walked the short distance to Wimpole Mews. Unfortunately, we found nothing of use to us. Several of the houses in the mews were used purely as surgeries, and therefore there had been no-one on the premises that night. The other residents had either taken a leaf from D Division's police surgeon's book, and taken their families to the seaside, or were dining out that evening. Several neighbours assured us that upon their return home there had been nothing out of the ordinary in the street. Several of them seemed to be quite disappointed by the fact. All of them said, however, that Dr. Simpson had been a quiet neighbour, as were his employees.

We walked back to Baker Street with Holmes sinking into a surly silence.

When we reached our rooms, Holmes headed for his violin. After several discordant scrapes of the bow across the strings, I chose to retreat to the dubious amenities of my club. I played a few games of billiards before returning home.

Mrs. Hudson, always able to sense when things were not going to plan, provided us with an excellent dinner to compensate. Creamy cucumber soup, followed by lamb chops accompanied by broad beans a la poulette, that is to say, broad beans cooked in stock with herbs, eggs, and cream and seasoned with salt and pepper, and boiled potatoes. It was not until we were on the last course of baked apple dumplings with cream that Holmes at last spoke.

"I do not like this."

"The dumplings?" I replied. "Why on earth not? They are delicious."

"I do not refer to the food, Watson, but to the case. I fear that this case is not going to be easy."

I put my spoon down and looked across the table at my friend's sombre expression.

He looked at me. "We have no clues, no motive, and no suspects. I have the horrid suspicion that there will be more murders."

"What can we do?"

"Nothing. We must wait."

"For another murder?" I asked fearfully.

"For another murder," he replied, his tone grim.

Chapter Four

We did not have long to wait. It was a mere two days before a constable was at our door relaying Lestrade's request for our attendance.

We accompanied the man back to Simpson's house in Wimpole Mews, where Lestrade was waiting outside for us, his expression shuttered.

"I take it that the victim is Caleb Evans?" were the first words Holmes said to Lestrade.

The little man nodded his head. "Though how you knew…"

"Withers told us," I said. "He said that Evans was going to remain here, but he was going to lodge with his mother in Putney."

"Pimlico," Holmes said.

"Pardon?" Lestrade blinked at us.

"Withers was returning to his mother in Pimlico, not Putney."

"It doesn't matter," Lestrade said wearily. He waved towards the door. "Come in."

We followed Lestrade into the house and out the back into the kitchen. As we walked Holmes asked Lestrade, "Who found the body?"

"Local constable. He was walking down the street and noticed the front door was standing slightly open. He knew about the murder of Dr. Simpson, of course. He wondered if some ghoul had broken in to see what he could steal, so he entered himself. When he found the body, he immediately went out on the street and blew his whistle for assistance. He remained here while the constable on the neighbouring beat ran to the station. The sergeant on duty sent for me."

A uniformed sergeant and two constables stood guard outside the kitchen door.

A tin bath sat in the middle of the kitchen floor. Fluid slopped over onto the polished black and white tiles. A man lay in the bath with his arms and legs dangling over the edges, and his head beneath the liquid. My nostrils twitched at the smell. It took me a moment to realize that what I was smelling was not bath water, but the yeast-sour scent of beer. Beer that was rapidly turning stale.

"Beer?" I said, astonishment in my voice. "He was drowned in beer?"

"It's a rum do, Doctor," said the sergeant. "First time I seen any bugger drowned in beer."

"Me grandad saw it once," one of the constables said. "He was on duty the night of the Beer Flood."

The Beer Flood had occurred on 17th October 1814 when wooden barrels of beer in the Horse Shoe Brewery belonging to Meux & Co had burst, smashing the walls and sending more than 100,000 gallons of fermenting dark beer, or porter, through the streets of St. Giles Rookery. At least eight people had drowned in the flood. Including members of a family gathered for the wake of a small child.

"Well, this drowning was most certainly not an accident," Holmes observed. He approached the bathtub. I followed him.

Holmes lifted one arm of the corpse, peeling back the grubby cuff of the shirt. Rope burns were clear on the skin. "No doubt we will find that these match the rope used on both Simpson and Cartwright."

Holmes was examining the abrasions with his magnifying lens, and then moved down from the wrists. "Look at his hands. Evans certainly put up a fight."

Lestrade and I leaned forward. I could clearly see that there were bruises and abrasions on the man's knuckles. Evans had clearly fought for him life but had been overpowered.

Holmes stopped, put his lens back into his pocket, and took the dead man's clenched fist into his hands. Gently, Holmes began to prise the fist open, giving a sharp cry of triumph as he managed to drag something from the dead man's grasp. It was a crumpled and torn piece of paper.

Holmes flattened it out. Lestrade and I gathered curiously to read it. It appeared to be written in some strange code. Odd little pictographs. I could not think why the dead man had clung to it in his death throws.

"Is it a code, Holmes?" Lestrade asked, his voice showing his puzzlement.

"Not exactly, Lestrade. It is a form of language. I have

come across it in my studies on codes and cyphers."

"Do you know what it is, and can you read it?" Lestrade asked, his tone hopeful.

"The answers to that are yes and no. Yes, I know what it is, but no, I cannot read it. However, I know who can."

Lestrade and I looked at each other then back at Holmes.

"Do not keep us in suspense, Holmes," I begged.

"It is a form of Ancient Egyptian known as hieroglyphics. There are several curators at the British Museum who will be able to translate it for us." Holmes carefully folded the paper and tucked it securely into the pocket of his waistcoat.

"Well then," said Lestrade, rubbing his hands together. "Why don't we make a visit?"

"Why not indeed?" I agreed.

The British Museum, situated in Great Russell Street, had its beginnings in the collection of Sir Hans Sloane, whom upon his death in 1753 deeded his collection to the government, in exchange for £20,000 to be given to his heirs. The politicians realized that this was quite a bargain, and they passed a bill that became known as the British Museum Act of 1753. The Act allowed for the setting up of a space where the public could enjoy Sir Hans Sloane's bequest in comfort and safety.

Moving extremely swiftly for politicians, a breed not known for fleetness of action, the Act received Royal Assent in

June 1753, and the first meeting of what was to become the trustees of the British Museum, took place in December 1753 at the Cockpit, Whitehall. Their first decision was where to situate the museum.

After much discussion they elected to purchase the long-neglected Montagu House in Bloomsbury. Noted architect Henry Keene was appointed to oversee the transformation from a rundown private residence into a museum.

Many prominent people donated prized items to the museum. In 1757 King George II donated most of the texts collected by his royal ancestors throughout the centuries. Much later his grandson, King George IV gave the library collected by his father King George III to the museum. These texts, and others donated, such as the Lindisfarne Gospels, formed the basis of the collection within the museum that could be accessed via the museum's Reading Room if one had membership.

After the Battle of the Nile in 1798, in which Lord Nelson and the British Navy defeated the French, Egyptian items began to filter back. Those who fought in the battle brought home ancient souvenirs which formed the basis of the museum's Egyptology collection.

In 1882 the British Museum joined with a number of other sponsors to create the Egypt Exploration Fund, which conducted a large number of expeditions each year, adding to the museum's vast collection. So vast that the museum now employed more curators in that section than in any other.

When we arrived at the museum, Lestrade despatched

one of the museum guides to fetch one of those curators.

A tall man, with dark curly hair, and warm brown eyes that held a lively curiosity, came towards us, a smile of welcome on his face. He introduced himself as Henry Cavanagh.

"What can I do for you gentlemen? I must admit I find myself at loss as to what a prominent Scotland Yard detective and a famous consulting detective and his assistant could want from one such as myself. Gerald," he indicated the guide with a wave of a hand, "...said you specifically asked for someone from the Egyptology department."

"We did," Lestrade confirmed. "We have a case that needs your expertise."

Cavanagh raised a thoughtful eyebrow. "I am intrigued. Please come this way, gentlemen." He led us away from the display halls and down several dim corridors, before opening a door into what was quite clearly an office.

I realized at once that in some aspects Cavanagh was a kindred spirit to Holmes. The office was not so much cluttered as crammed to the gills with all sorts of oddments. Piles of paper sat haphazardly on a large desk. Books were stacked on chairs, and strange little figurines and carved stones littered the shelves of the cases that one would have expected the books to be sitting on.

"Come in. Take a seat." Cavanagh paused, looked around his office, looked at us slightly abashed, and hurried to remove the books from the several chairs that sat before the desk. The books were carefully piled on the floor in front of the bookcases.

When we had sat down, Cavanagh took his own seat and gazed at us expectantly across the paper strewn desk. "Now, what can I do for you gentlemen? Pray do not keep me in suspense."

Lestrade looked at Holmes, who nodded for him to speak. Lestrade took a deep breath. "We have had three murders. All very strange. All linked to one household. All obviously committed by more than one person." He looked at Holmes again. This time Holmes took pity on him.

"We had no motive, no suspects, and, until this morning no clues."

"But you have found something?" Cavanagh asked. "Something that brought you to me?"

"We did," Holmes confirmed. "A torn scrap of paper bearing Egyptian hieroglyphics. I recognized them for what they were, but, alas, I am unable to read them."

"I can most certainly do that for you," Cavanagh said. "And for that we can thank the French."

"The French?" I asked.

Cavanagh nodded. "One French man in particular, Jean-Francois Champollion. He deciphered the Rosetta Stone, which we have here in the museum. Have you seen it?"

I admitted that I had not. Visiting museums was not my favourite form of pastime.

"It is marvellous," Cavanagh enthused. "I shall show it to you before you leave. Champollion realized that the hieroglyphics recorded the sound of the ancient Egyptian language and was able to use the Greek and Egyptian demotic inscriptions that are also present on the stone to translate them. It opened up Egyptian history to us in an extraordinary way."

He smiled at us with happy expression of a man who has a captive audience for his favourite subject. For a moment he truly reminded me of Holmes.

Cavanagh held out his hand. "May I see the paper?"

"Of course." Holmes removed it from his breast pocket and handed it across the desk.

Cavanagh took the paper and gently smoothed it flat on his desk. He studied it for a moment, his brows creasing in concentration. After a while he looked up. "This is really quite extraordinary."

"You can read it?" Lestrade asked hopefully.

"Yes. And I recognize it."

"You do?" Holmes leaned forward expectantly.

"A year or so ago an archaeologist discovered a burial ground not far from Cairo. Not one for pharaohs or their wives, but one that has, in some respects, proved to be far more interesting. The archaeologist named it the Valley of the Magicians."

"Valley of the Magicians?" I asked.

37

"Sounds far more romantic than the Valley of the Priests, but it is, essentially, the burial ground for the priesthood of the god Ra. Ra's cult was prominent in the city of On or as the Greeks called it, Heliopolis. Today it is covered by a suburb of Cairo."

"Why call it the Valley of the Magicians if those buried in it were priests?" Lestrade asked.

"Magic was part and parcel of everyday life in ancient Egypt," Cavanagh replied. "What we would, if we were so inclined, ascribe to miracles, the Egyptians considered to be magic performed by the gods. And the first God of Magic was Ra. Though magic itself was considered a god. At the time the necropolis was started, Ra was the preeminent god. Later he became fused with the god Amun and was known as Amun-Ra." Cavanagh looked down at the paper on the desk. "This is part of the beginning of an inscription that was found in the most interesting tomb in the valley."

"What does it say?" I asked.

"In English, the first line reads 'I am Neb-Hek'. The second line says, 'First among'."

"Not particularly helpful," Lestrade observed.

Holmes was watching Cavanagh closely. "Patience, Lestrade. I do believe Mr. Cavanagh knows what the full inscription is."

Cavanagh chuckled. "I do indeed, Mr. Holmes." He hunted through the mounds of paper on his desk, before emerging with a notebook. "I have the full translation in here. I assume you wish to hear it?"

Holmes indicated on behalf of us all that this was so.

Cavanagh opened the book, cleared his throat several times, and began to read in a firm, deep, voice, that lent an eerie quality to the words:

"I am Neb-Heka-Ra –

First among Magicians –

First Servant of Ra.

I have treated no man unjustly.

I have had compassion for the widow and the orphan.

I have not eaten that which I should not.

Nor performed any act that is unclean.

No man can say of me: 'He has harmed me.'

I dwell now in my House of Eternity.

I declaim now that my curse shall fall upon he who disturbs my rest.

I call upon the gods to witness and avenge such impiety:

May the Sands of Set fill his nostrils;

May the Waters of Hapi enclose his head;

May the Beer of Tenenet strangle his throat;

May the Crocodile of Sobek rend his flesh;

May the Cobra of Uajyt strike his heel;

May the Vulture of Nekhbet tear his liver;

May the Blessed Lady Ma'at judge his soul;

May Nehebkau cause his Ka and Ba to separate;

And may Ammit devour his Heart – thus destroying him forever."

I freely admit that the hair on the back of my neck stood up as the words echoed around the room. Lestrade too seemed discomforted by the words. Only Holmes was unmoved by the dreadful curse that seemed to linger in the air around us.

"Interesting," Holmes murmured. "And informative."

"Informative?" Lestrade asked.

"Come now, Lestrade," Holmes said, somewhat testily. "Surely you noticed the first three lines of the actual curse?"

It took me a moment, still disturbed as I was, to grasp what Holmes meant. Then I gasped aloud. "The sands of Set, the waters of Hapi, and the beer of Tenenet."

"Exactly," said Holmes.

Cavanagh gave us a quizzical look. "The curse of Neb-Heka-Ra seems to mean something to you," he observed.

Lestrade, colour returning to his face, nodded emphatically. "Indeed, Mr. Cavanagh. I am unsure whether you have seen the newspapers regarding the death of Dr. Horace Simpson?"

Cavanagh nodded. "From memory the papers said he was murdered, but not how."

"His head was buried in a mound of sand," Lestrade replied.

Cavanagh caught on immediately. "The sands of Set. But the others?"

"Simpson had two assistants," Holmes said. "One was fished out of the Thames. The other was found this morning drowned in a bathtub full of beer."

Cavanagh sat back in his chair, clearly astounded by the revelations. "But who? And why?"

"That, my dear sir, is something we need to discover," Holmes replied.

"Who knows about the curse?" Lestrade asked.

Cavanagh scratched his chin thoughtfully. "The archaeologist who discovered the tomb, of course, and possibly his secretary. Then there would be the man who paid for the expedition and the man who expedited the removal of the mummy from Egypt."

"And these men are?" Lestrade had his notebook out.

"The archaeologist was Bernard Barrett. I can give you an address for him. I do not know who financed the expedition. Barrett was a little cagey about it. I only became aware of the existence of the mummy itself after it was delivered here after its unwrapping." His tone carried deep disapproval.

"Unwrapping?" Lestrade looked up from his notebook.

"Some men who finance expeditions feel they need to get more out of it than the possibility of being a footnote in some learned paper." Cavanagh's voice was tight. "So, they take the mummy and hold unwrapping parties in the hopes that the mummy might have amulets of precious and semiprecious stones that they can claim. It is, quite frankly, a rather macabre version of the children's game of 'Pass the Parcel.'"

Cavanagh sighed. "In the early days it was much more scientific. Thomas Pettigrew's unwrappings were more about what could be learned from the mummy, not what could be gained from it monetarily. These days the parties are extremely rare as we have fewer people of means financing private expeditions."

"But it still occurs," Holmes said.

"Yes. As to the facilitator," Cavanagh continued, "I believe Barrett most likely used a Frenchman, one Thierry Meylan, who was based in Cairo." Cavanagh paused and frowned, "Though I heard from a colleague in Italy that the man died suddenly whilst visiting his operation there."

"Is that normal," Lestrade asked. "To operate in two different countries like that?"

"Oh yes," Cavanagh said, "Especially if there is smuggling going on."

"Smuggling?" Holmes asked.

"The Egyptian government is, quite naturally, annoyed

at the number of their historical treasures being syphoned into Europe. They have quite strict limits on what can and cannot be sent out of the country. Men like Thierry Meylan simply ignore that in favour of lining their own pockets. Antiquities are simply smuggled out, usually to Italy, where the government is corrupt enough to hold out their hands for payment and look the other way. Usually simultaneously." Cavanagh sighed, and dug through the papers on his desk again, before coming up with a business card. He handed it to Lestrade. "Barrett's address."

Lestrade carefully copied the details into his notebook before handing the card back to Cavanagh.

"Is there anything else I can help you gentlemen with?" Cavanagh asked.

Lestrade shook his head. "You have been most helpful."

"Come then, I shall show you out, but first you might like to see Neb-Heka-Ra himself, and I did promise to show Doctor Watson the Rosetta Stone."

Holmes held up a hand. "If I may have a copy of the curse? That would be most useful."

"Of course, Mr. Holmes. I shall bring a copy around to your rooms in Baker Street later today."

I got the feeling that Henry Cavanagh wanted an excuse to visit. Holmes must have felt that too, assuring Cavanagh that we would expect him later that afternoon.

Cavanagh then guided us further back into the labyrinthine rooms away from the public's gaze. He took us into a room remarkably similar to a morgue, with its walls lined with heavy cadaver drawers.

Selecting a drawer towards the middle of the back wall, he opened it, displaying its contents for us to see.

The desiccated remains of what had once been a man looked up at us. One arm had detached at the shoulder and lay loosely on his chest, which was sunken. I could see that many of the ribs were broken. The feet had detached at the ankles and sat oddly at attention at the end of the drawer. Holmes moved close to the drawer and began to inspect the remains, paying particular attention, I noticed, to the desiccated head. He seemed to be absorbed in taking note of the mummy's facial features.

Cavanagh gazed down at the corpse sadly. "An enormous amount of damage was done by the unwrapping. We will probably never be able to display him for the public. The man who unwrapped him, practically butchered him. Mummies need to be handled gently, otherwise things like this happen." He gestured at the violated corpse sadly. "A sorry end for a distinguished man. Probably a High Priest of Ra."

"How can you know he was a High Priest?" I asked curiously.

"By his name. It is unlikely to be his birth name. The name reflects power. Neb means lord, Heka means magic, and Ra is a god. Therefore Neb-Heka-Ra translates into something like "Lord of the Magic of Ra".

"Not a name you would give a child," Lestrade

observed.

"Egyptian pharaohs usually had a regnal name," Cavanagh explained. "Take Thutmoses the Great, for example. One of Egypt's greatest warrior kings. His birth name was Menkhperre – Eternal are the Manifestations of Ra."

"No different I suppose from our queen," Lestrade observed. "She was Princess Alexandrina Victoria but chose to reign simply as Victoria".

Cavanagh beamed at him. "Exactly, Inspector."

Closing the drawer, Cavanagh led us back out into the public areas of the museum. There were already quite a number of people perusing the exhibits as we were led to the Egyptology department.

Standing on a plinth was a block of polished black granite, almost four feet tall and over two feet wide. The block was covered in what was quite clearly three different forms of writing.

"The Rosetta Stone, gentlemen," said Cavanagh. "It tells an interesting tale."

"What does it say?" asked Lestrade.

"It records the benefits conferred on the priesthood by Ptolemy V in 196 BC," Cavanagh replied. "Ptolemy needed to appease them after they supported a rebellion against him that almost succeeded. The rebellion had been led by a native Egyptian named Ankhwennefre who desired to see a native dynasty back in power. Ptolemy was Greek, as I am sure you know."

We nodded dutifully.

Cavanagh smiled. "It's an interesting piece of history. The rebellion frightened Ptolemy badly, hence the gifts, and concessions, he gave to the various priesthoods. But the most interesting thing about the stele is the languages those concessions are recorded in."

Here Cavanagh pointed at the stone. "It is those languages that eventually allowed for us to translate the inscriptions on the tombs, and the curse which you heard earlier. The stone is inscribed in Greek, Egyptian demotic, and Egyptian hieroglyphics. Champollion, whom I mentioned before, realized that hieroglyphics were also a language, as I also mentioned. It's not the only stone of its type around, but the Rosetta Stone is certainly the most famous. It will still be talked about a hundred years from now."

"Fascinating," I murmured. It truly was. I was no stranger to native revolts, having served in Afghanistan.

We said farewell to Henry Cavanagh and left the British Museum in a subdued frame of mind.

We were standing in Great Russell Street when Lestrade said, "I honestly cannot see any link between an unwrapped mummy and the murders."

Holmes raised his eyebrows. "Can you not?"

"No, I cannot. I can see the link to the curse. That is as plain as the nose on your face. But why?"

"Who better to unwrap a mummy, Lestrade, than a surgeon?"

I looked at Holmes. "You think Simpson did the unwrapping?"

"I think it is highly probable," Holmes replied. "No doubt Mr. Bernard Barrett will be able to tell us who butchered that ancient corpse."

I winced at the memory. "It was not done well at all, was it?"

"No, it was not. Come now. Lestrade, you have Barrett's address?"

Lestrade held up his notebook. "I do."

"Then let us head to his lodgings and see what he has to tell us upon the subject of mummies and murders," Holmes said.

Chapter Five

Bernard Barrett lived in a suite of rooms close by University College, London. The university had recently set up an Egyptology department to house the collection of well-known novelist and Egyptologist, Amelia Edwards. Noted archaeologist William Matthew Flinders Petrie was currently head of the department and conducted many important excavations in Egypt. It made sense that Barrett would lodge close to both Petrie and the British Museum. Though I had formed the opinion that Henry Cavanagh was less than impressed with Mr. Barrett.

Bernard Barrett's rooms were located in Huntly Street. A weary looking landlady let us in to the building and led us upstairs where she rapped sharply upon a door. "Mr. Barrett. Some gentlemen from Scotland Yard to see you."

The door was opened by a thin, hollow-cheeked, man, with soulful brown eyes that leant him a startling resemblance to a spaniel that had just been kicked. He nodded to the lady. "Thank you, Mrs. Hastings."

Mrs. Hastings turned and headed back down the stairs. The man stepped back from the door and opened it wide. "What can Mr. Barrett do for Scotland Yard today?"

I raised my eyebrows slightly at the odd mode of speech.

"Mr. Barrett," Lestrade began.

The man shook his head. "I am not Mr. Barrett. I am Joseph Brown, Mr. Barrett's secretary. Please. Come in."

We followed Joseph Brown into what was clearly a study. Two walls were lined from floor to ceiling with bookcases that were crammed with all manner of books, journals, and odd little bits of stone and pottery. I noticed many of these last items were engraved with what I had learned were hieroglyphics. A solid oak desk sat in front of the solitary window.

Seated at the desk was a lean, but muscular man, with sharp-chiselled features, and equally sharp eyes. He turned away from his writing to look at us as Brown showed us into the room.

"Joseph," the seated man snapped. "I told you that I did not wish to be disturbed."

"I am aware of that, Mr. Barrett, however, these gentlemen are from Scotland Yard…"

"I don't care if they are from Mars! I told you…"

"Mr. Barrett," Lestrade cut coldly across what appeared to be building up into a tirade. "Your secretary obviously has more sense than you. If Scotland Yard comes calling, we are obviously not here for a cup of tea and a chin wag!"

Barrett stopped, mouth hanging open, and looked at Lestrade in some shock. It was obvious that the man was not used to being spoken to in such a manner. He took a moment to collect himself before saying, in a smooth, slightly unctuous, tone, "My apologies, gentlemen, who are you and what exactly can I do for you today?"

"I am Inspector Lestrade of Scotland Yard." Lestrade gestured to us. "This is Mr. Sherlock Holmes and Dr. John Watson."

Barrett rose to his feet and shook our hands. "I have heard of all three of you. I am an avid reader of Dr. Watson's stories in *Strand Magazine*. They have beguiled away many a dull night while on a dig."

I inclined my head in thanks and sat down in one of the chairs that Brown had hurriedly provided for us.

"As for what you can do for us…" Lestrade gestured to Holmes to take up the story.

"Mr. Barrett," my friend said. "Are you aware of the recent murders that have taken place?"

"Which ones?" Barrett replied.

"The murder of Dr. Horace Simpson and his two assistants."

Barrett gaped at us. "Simpson has been murdered?"

"He was found in his study suffocated with sand."

"I saw in the papers that a man had been found dead in extremely odd circumstances in Wimpole Mews. I did not realize that it was Simpson." Barrett shook his head. "And his assistants too, you say?"

"Yes. One was drowned in water and discovered in the Thames." Holmes paused and looked at Barrett closely before continuing, "The second was found drowned in a bathtub full of beer."

Barrett blinked. "But that is absurd. Why on...?" He paused. We could see the light of understanding dawn on his face. "That damn curse."

"The Curse of Neb-Heka-Ra," Holmes stated.

Barrett nodded. "I have read, and seen, some strange and eerie things in my travels in Egypt, but that curse..." His voice trailed off. "My native workers nearly rioted when the tomb was found with that curse on it. I had to pay triple wages to get any of them to continue to work. It is all nonsense of course, even in the ancient times many tombs were raided without supernatural retribution."

"There is nothing supernatural about these murders," Holmes stated firmly.

Barrett raised his eyebrows in query.

"I very much doubt that such uncanny entities as might be invoked by a curse need to bind their victims with rope," Holmes said dryly.

Barrett understood immediately. "Then the killer or killers comes from a very narrow circle."

"Such people who knew about the curse," my friend said.

"Exactly," replied Barrett.

"And who would they be?" Lestrade asked, drawing his notebook from his pocket.

"Myself, of course, my secretary, Joseph Brown, whom you just met. Cavanagh at the British Museum."

"We met him," I said. "He is the man who gave us your address."

"And a lecture on the Rosetta Stone, no doubt," Barrett said, with a slight smile.

"He is certainly enthusiastic about his work," was my non-committal reply.

"Did Simpson know about the curse?" Lestrade asked.

Barrett shook his head. "No. He wasn't interested in Egypt. The unwrapping was simply a job for him. He unwrapped Neb-Heka-Ra, and I supplied a commentary on what was being displayed as he did so."

"Where did the unwrapping take place?" Lestrade asked.

"At the town house of Lord Reginald Ashmoore, on..." Barrett stopped, rummaged around on his desk, coming up with a small appointment book. He opened it, flicked through it, and then handed the opened book to Lestrade. "...this day."

Holmes looked over Lestrade's shoulder. "I shall have to double check, but I fancy that is the same day and time as one of the appointments in Simpson's appointment book."

"I cannot tell you who the guests were. I did not recognize any of them. I don't move in those circles, and Lord Reginald did not introduce me to anyone. If it hadn't been for Simpson and his assistants, I would not have had anyone to speak to." Barrett's expression was bitter. "I was basically a servant, like those serving the food and drinks." The expression twisted into a grimace that may have been an attempt at a wry smile. "For all his pretensions, Simpson was in exactly the same situation. Ashmoore viewed him as hired help." He paused. "There was one woman though, the wife of a banker. Asked the most impertinent and dubious questions."

"There was nothing scientific about this unwrapping, then?" Holmes asked, his expression intent.

Barrett shook his head. "It was theatre, pure and simple, Mr. Holmes. He even set the mood before the show started."

"How?" Holmes asked.

"Ashmoore employed an actor to recite the curse before Simpson began the unwrapping. I have to admit, it did make the atmosphere in the room somewhat eerie."

"So, any of the guests would know of the curse," Lestrade said.

Barrett stopped for a moment, looking abashed. "Yes," he said slowly, "I suppose they would."

"Then the suspect list is quite a bit larger than you originally assumed," Lestrade said.

Barrett nodded slowly. "Yes. I suppose it is."

"Who financed the expedition?" Holmes asked.

"Lord Ashmoore, of course. Though I believe the banker chap, Wilson, also put up a fair bit of dosh. But it was Lord Ashmoore's venture from start to finish. Hence his hosting the unwrapping," Barrett replied.

"You have Lord Reginald Ashmoore's address," Holmes stated rather than asked.

Barrett nodded again and then hunted around in his desk before coming up with an elegant calling card. Lestrade took it and wrote the details down in his notebook.

As we turned to leave, Holmes turned back to Barrett. "Was your secretary present at the unwrapping?"

"Joseph? No. He did make the arrangements with Ashmoore's secretary, but there was no need for him to be present."

Holmes nodded and we left. Outside in the street, Lestrade checked his fob-watch. "It is getting too late now to call on Lord Ashmoore. I shall send a note around with a constable and arrange a time for tomorrow, if that suits you gentlemen?"

"It does," Holmes replied. "In any case we are expecting Mr. Cavanagh to call later today with a copy of the curse."

Lestrade nodded and got into the police growler that was waiting at the curb. "Can I give you gentlemen a lift home?"

Holmes shook his head. "It is close enough to Baker Street for us to walk. Have a good afternoon, Lestrade. We shall see you tomorrow." With that, he walked away, leaving me to scurry after him.

I knew Holmes wanted to sort through what we had

learned today, so I refrained from attempting conversation as we walked back to Baker Street. The day was pleasant enough. Warm, with a light breeze that stopped it from being too uncomfortable for such gentle exercise as we were undertaking.

We could hear Mrs. Hudson in her kitchen when we returned, and the succulent smells emanating from it promised an excellent dinner. That good lady popped her head out when she heard us.

"I was beginning to think you would not make it back for dinner."

"What is for dinner?" I asked.

"I got some excellent sausages from the butcher this morning. Which will be served with potatoes in onion gravy, and boiled artichokes. I have made you a Delhi pudding for afters."

I licked my lips. I was quite fond of Delhi pudding, which was an apple pudding made with a suet crust and flavoured with sugar, minced lemon peel, and currants.

"A fine feast indeed," Holmes said, with a slight smile at my reaction. "But before dinner we will require tea and perhaps a few of your excellent biscuits. We are expecting a visitor before dinner."

"Tea and biscuits it shall be then, Mr. Holmes," our landlady replied.

"Thank you, Mrs. Hudson."

We continued up the stairs to our flat.

Chapter Six

It was around an hour later that Mrs. Hudson showed Henry Cavanagh into the flat.

The jovial curator handed over copies of the curse even as he took the seat Holmes ushered him to. "I wrote out a copy for each of you gentlemen." Cavanagh seemed eager to please.

"I thank you kindly," Holmes said. "You will take tea with us?"

"I would be delighted." Cavanagh fairly beamed with pleasure.

I wondered what on Earth Holmes was up to. The man was not one for unnecessary chit-chat and I thought that he would have obtained such knowledge as he required from Cavanagh when we were at the museum.

Mrs. Hudson brought in the tea, with plates of her excellent shortbread and ginger biscuits. Holmes took the tray from her, placing in on the table, and poured tea for the three of us.

Cavanagh took one each of the offered biscuits, settling himself comfortably in the chair. He glanced around the room in obvious pleasure.

Holmes took a sip of his tea before saying "We spoke with Mr. Barrett. A rather abrupt gentleman, but he told us that the mummy was unwrapped at Lord Reginald Ashmoore's London home. The man also provided much of the finance for the expedition to Egypt."

Cavanagh snorted. "That would make sense. Lord Ashmoore keeps trying to weasel his way onto the body of the Egypt Exploration Fund. He has very little practical knowledge and a highly inflated opinion of what little he does have. The man irritates those with genuine knowledge and experience. I do not like him. William Petrie once described him as a 'bombastic buffoon.' I am afraid that I agree with him." He smiled wryly, "And Lord Ashmoore does not like me either. He is also trying to get on to the Board of Trustees for the museum. I keep blocking him. Not personally, you understand, but those on the board trust my judgment where Egyptology and Egyptologists are concerned."

"Then why did he gift the mummy to the museum?" I asked.

Holmes looked at me in some amusement. "What else was he to do with it, my dear Watson? Unwrapped it is, unfortunately, merely a pile of bones and preserved flesh. Not something I warrant most people would care to keep in their home."

"Not even Lord Ashmoore," Cavanagh agreed.

"You mentioned amulets when we visited earlier," Holmes said. "I am curious about them."

Cavanagh raised his eyebrows in silent query.

"We have to find a murderer, Mr. Cavanagh, and to find him we need a motive. Valuable amulets could provide a motive," Holmes explained.

Cavanagh looked thoughtful.

"Why did the Egyptians put amulets on mummies?" I asked.

"To keep them safe and to protect them on their journey to the Field of Reeds."

"Field of Reeds?"

"The Ancient Egyptian heaven if you will. The place of residence in the afterlife."

"They seem to have been obsessed with death," I commented.

"More like obsessed with life," Cavanagh said. "An Egyptian could think of nothing finer than continuing to live well in another plane of existence. To laugh and love, hunt and dance, feast and celebrate for all eternity. The amulets helped with that."

"How so?" Holmes asked.

"The amulets were carefully placed throughout the wrappings to act as protection and to provide instructions on safely navigating the passage to Iaru, which is the Egyptian name for the Field of Reeds. There were many obstacles to overcome before they reached there. The last being having to face the tribunal where their acts in this life where judged."

I had to admit that I was fascinated. "How were they judged?" I asked.

"The heart of the deceased was weighed against the

feather of truth in the presence of the gods. If the heart weighed more that the feather, the deceased was judged unworthy, and the heart thrown to the demon-god, Ammit, who ate it." Cavanagh paused. "In the words of the curse 'thus destroying him forever.'"

Words from my childhood visits to church came back to me. "Mene, mene, tekel upharsin: thou art weighed in the balances and art found wanting," I murmured.

"The book of Daniel, I believe," Holmes said. "Very fitting, Watson.

Cavanagh nodded his agreement. "Fitting indeed."

Holmes turned back to Cavanagh. "So, the amulets were valuable. Were they made of valuable materials?"

Cavanagh shook his head. "Not really. Most amulets were made of glass or faience."

"Faience?" I asked.

"A ceramic made of crushed quartz or sand with small amounts of calcite lime and alkalis," Cavanagh replied. "A glaze using copper was employed to colour them blue and green. Much ornamentation was made from faience. Other amulets were made from haematite, carnelian, and jasper. Not gemstones that would be conventionally thought of as valuable. To the Egyptians the value was in what the amulet represented."

"And that was?" Holmes asked.

"The value was mostly in the shape and the colour. Green and blue amulets represented rebirth into the afterlife, red ones symbolized blood, strength, and power. Those made in the shape of the Eye of Ra protected the wearer against all evils. We often find those throughout mummy wrappings." Cavanagh paused. "People often approach the museum hoping to purchase genuine amulets."

I was astounded. "What on earth for?"

"Many people still believe in the veracity of amulets, Dr. Watson."

I could not forebear snorting. "Load of tommyrot!"

"Is it?" Cavanagh asked, raising an eyebrow at my vehemence. "How does it differ from, say, a St. Christopher Medal or a string of rosary beads to a Roman Catholic? Or carrying a rabbit's foot for good luck? Or the habit of placing a lock of hair from a deceased person in a locket?" He suddenly grinned. "Or, for that matter, the sovereign that Mr. Holmes has attached to his watch chain?"

I stared at him, unable to respond.

Cavanagh's grin got wider. "I read the Bohemia story in the *Strand Magazine*." He was suddenly serious again, as he said quietly, "They are all amulets, Doctor, it is just that we do not call them such, anymore."

"One thing is clear," Holmes said, cutting smoothly into the conversation, looking up from the paper in his hand. He had been reading the curse as we had conversed. "Such amulets as were upon the mummy are not the motive for the murders."

"Then what is the motive?" I asked curiously.

"Revenge," Holmes replied.

"Revenge?" I asked.

"You saw the state of the remains of Neb-Heka-Ra, Watson. Someone is out for revenge for what they see as an act of desecration; of sacrilege, almost."

"But whom?"

"That, my dear Watson, is what we need to find out." He turned to our guest. "Mr. Cavanagh, my thanks for the copies of the curse and for your conversation. It has been most enlightening."

Cavanagh took the hint and rose to his feet. "Thank you for tea. If I can be of further assistance, you know where to find me." He bowed slightly to us and took his leave.

Cavanagh had been gone about ten minutes, when Mrs. Hudson showed another visitor into our rooms.

It was a man, slightly under six feet in height, sharp brown eyes, dark hair and moustache, and the warm olive complexion of one who was from the Mediterranean area. He bowed slightly to us both. "My apologies for arriving without an appointment, gentlemen. My name is Abasi Tarek."

Holmes waved his hand towards a chair. "Please, take a seat Mr. Tarek, and tell Dr. Watson and myself what it is that brings you here."

"I am here in London on the behest of the Khedive of

Egypt, the great Abbas II Helmy Bay. My usual employment is to facilitate the importing of British manufactured goods to my country and to arrange the export of our excellent agricultural products in return."

He handed his card to Holmes. I looked over Holmes's shoulder at the card, which was engraved with Tarek's name, an address on the Strand, and the words 'Importer/Exporter by Appointment of the Khedive of Egypt.'

Holmes looked up from the card to our guest. "Your usual employment, you say?"

Abasi Tarek smiled briefly. "You are as quick as they say, Mr. Holmes. I have been given a special commission by the Khedive."

"And that is?"

"To discover what has occurred with the mummy of Neb-Heka-Ra and what has happened to the goods from his tomb."

"Why would this be of interest to the Khedive?" I asked.

"What do you know of archaeology, Dr. Watson?" Tarek asked.

"Nothing at all," I admitted.

"Know then that when permission is given to excavate a tomb, an arrangement is made for only a few items to actually be removed from Egypt. The archaeologist Bernard Barrett was granted an excavation permit that allowed him to take only duplicate items from the tomb. The mummy was to remain in

Cairo."

"Mr. Cavanagh from the British Museum mentioned there is much smuggling," I said.

"Mr. Henry Cavanagh is correct," Tarek said. "In this instance, the government agent who was overseeing the dig received a message saying his father was dreadfully ill in their village some sixty miles from Cairo. Naturally, he hastened to his father's bedside."

Holmes gave Abasi Tarek a shrewd look. "But the man was not ill?"

"No, he was not. It was a ruse to get him away. By the time he returned, Barrett and his party had gone, as had the mummy of Neb-Heka-Ra and all his grave goods. Also missing was a Frenchman by the name of Thierry Meylan."

Holmes nodded. "Cavanagh mentioned him. I believe he said that he was the man most likely to have arranged for the mummy to be removed."

"He also mentioned that he had heard that Meylan had died in Italy," I said.

Abasi Tarek gave me a startled look. "I had not heard that, Dr. Watson. Thank you for telling me. I must send word to the Khedive." He turned back to my friend. "I understand that you are investigating murders that are linked to the curse of Neb-Heka-Ra."

"Where did you hear that?" I asked.

"I am not a fool, Dr. Watson. The famous Sherlock

Holmes visits the British Museum to speak to an expert on ancient Egypt after being seen at the scenes of three strange, but brutal, deaths? One does not have to be a detective oneself to realize that these things are linked."

Holmes chuckled drily. "Well done, Mr. Tarek. I take it you wish me to discover exactly what has happened to the contents of Neb-Heka-Ra's tomb? We do know what happened to the mummy, after all."

Tarek sighed. "Dumped like so much garbage on the British Museum I understand. Will you please investigate for us, Mr Holmes? If it is not too much trouble. The Khedive will reward you."

Holmes waved a hand. "I am sure the whereabouts of the goods will become obvious once we discover where the mummy of Neb-Heka-Ra was unwrapped and who financed the expedition. I shall pass that information on to you for the Khedive."

Tarek rose to his feet. "Thank you, Mr. Holmes. I appreciate your assistance with this matter." He nodded politely to us both and took his leave.

I walked to the window and watched Tarek hail a cab in the street. Holmes came and joined me.

"Why did you not tell him that we knew who was behind both the money for the excavation and the unwrapping?" I asked.

Holmes chuckled drily. "I am afraid that it quite slipped

my mind, my dear Watson."

I snorted. "A likely tale indeed."

"Abasi Tarek did not need to know that information at this point. I am not about to start handing over information when I do not know where someone fits in the scheme of things. Until we know more, I would prefer to keep Mr. Tarek in the dark." He turned towards me. "I believe a visit to Mycroft is now on the agenda."

"To find out more about Abasi Tarek?"

"Indeed."

"Will we go to his office before we join Lestrade on visiting Lord Ashmoore?"

Holmes pulled thoughtfully on his lower lip. "No. I do not think so. I think it would be better to go to the Diogenes Club tomorrow evening, after we have seen everyone who attended the unwrapping. Mycroft may well have more information on the other people involved as well as the interesting Mr. Tarek."

Chapter Seven

Lestrade arrived at our rooms early the next morning as we were having breakfast. Mrs. Hudson hastened to fetch him a plate, and at her urging he filled it with devilled kidneys, poached eggs, and bacon. Lestrade ate with evident enjoyment before relaxing and joining us in a cup of coffee. Holmes was partial to coffee with breakfast, and I had become accustomed to it over the years. It was an invigorating drink to start the day with.

As we drank our coffee, Holmes filled Lestrade in on the two visits the previous day.

"Cavanagh's not wrong on amulets," Lestrade observed. "I know a lot of officers who carry a lucky piece of some description. Gregson keeps a button from off his first uniform as a constable in his breast pocket." He took a sip of his coffee. "This Abasi Tarek...could he be the killer?"

Holmes frowned. "It is possible," he conceded.

"But you have your doubts," I observed.

"Indeed." Holmes leaned back in his seat. "While it is not unheard of for a criminal to attempt to involve himself in an investigation, I deem it unlikely in this instance."

"Why so?" I asked.

"According to his card, and his own words, Abasi Tarek is an official representative of the Khedive of Egypt. Such a man, while probably not scrupling at committing murder, would not go out of his way to draw attention to himself. To do so would risk drawing condemnation from his own government."

Lestrade placed his cup down on the table. "Well then, gentlemen, perhaps we should start on our calls for the day?"

We hailed a cab and headed out to Chiswick. Lord Reginald Ashmoore had a house on Chiswick Mall, a street of fine houses that faced the Thames.

Chiswick was an old area, with settlement going back to prehistoric times. The name itself came from the Old English word 'ceswican' meaning cheese farm. Indeed, until the 18th century an annual cheese fair was held in a field near the river known as Duke's Meadow. Though the name gives the impression that the area is rural, it is less so now. It is only about six miles from Chiswick to inner London and rich men have been making it their home since Tudor times, or earlier.

Lord Ashmoore's house was a fine 17th century house built in the Palladian style favoured by Inigo Jones. With sweeping columns lining the front, it looked more like the temple of a Greek god, than the home of an Englishman.

A liveried butler answered our knock, and upon hearing our errand, escorted us into a study and left to fetch Lord Reginald.

The study was a furnished with a heavy mahogany desk with a matching chair. A large window looked out over the Thames. Several bookcases lined the walls and were crammed with books on archaeology and Egypt. A glass and walnut cabinet held pottery and pieces of carved rock. I went over to look. The carvings appeared to be hieroglyphs, such as Cavanagh had shown us. I wondered if the items had come from the tomb of Neb-Heka-Ra.

The door opened to admit a man of late middle age. He was tall, thin to the point of being cadaverous, with mouse-brown hair that was fading to grey. Sharp brown eyes rested on Holmes before flicking to Lestrade and myself.

"My man says that you are from Scotland Yard and wish to talk to me about the mummy unwrapping?" His tone held disbelief.

"That is correct, Lord Ashmoore," Lestrade said. "I am Inspector Lestrade from Scotland Yard. This is Mr. Sherlock Holmes and Doctor John Watson, who are assisting the Yard with our investigation into several murders."

"I fail to see what my mummy unwrapping has to do with murders, but come gentlemen, let us go to the library. There really is not room in here to sit and discuss such matters."

As the only chair in the room was the one at the desk, we could really only agree and follow him from the room.

His Lordship led us up a flight of stairs and into a large, well-lit, library. The bookcases here were much older than those in the study, being 18th century glass fronted cases. It was obvious that the library contained the book collections of several generations of Ashmoores.

Comfortable armchairs were scattered around the room.

Lord Ashmoore gestured for us to be seated.

"Now, what is all this nonsense about the mummy unwrapping and murders?"

"It is not nonsense, Lord Ashmoore," Lestrade said. "Three men have been found murdered, and they all have a connection to the mummy unwrapping. As do the murders themselves."

Lord Ashmoore snorted inelegantly. "I highly doubt that! Rest assured I will be complaining about your cheek in coming here to the Commissioner himself."

"The Commissioner is well aware that we are here, Lord Ashmoore," Holmes said coldly. "He will be less than pleased with your lack of cooperation."

Lord Ashmoore spluttered in fury, his voice rising to a shout. "Now look here you…"

"No!" my friend said sharply. "You look here! Dr. Horace Simpson and his two assistants who unwrapped the mummy of Neb-Heka-Ra at your wretched party are dead. All three undeniably murdered. One suffocated with sand, one drowned and then thrown into the Thames, and the third drowned in beer."

Lord Ashmoore choked; his anger being drowned by his astonishment. "The curse," he whispered.

"Exactly," snapped Holmes.

The door opened at that moment and a fashionably dressed woman entered the room. She was wearing a morning gown of green silk that rustled pleasantly as she walked. Her ebony black hair was artfully arranged, and her warm brown eyes held concern. She was much younger than Lord Reginald Ashmoore, and I took her to be his daughter, until she spoke.

"Reginald, what on earth are you yelling about? You know the doctor does not want you getting upset. It is not good for you." Her accent was slightly foreign, but I could not place it.

Lord Ashmoore looked contrite. "I am sorry, my dear. I let my temper get the better of me."

She turned to look at us, then back at the man who was obviously her husband. "Who are these men?"

"My dear, may I introduce Inspector Lestrade of Scotland Yard, Mr. Sherlock Holmes, and Dr. John Watson." He turned to us. "Gentlemen, this is my wife, Lady Veronica Ashmoore."

"A pleasure to meet you, Lady Ashmoore," Lestrade said, with a slight bow. "You have our apologies for disturbing your household."

"My household is not disturbed, inspector, only my husband." She smiled briefly. For a moment she looked so exotic and so beautiful that she took my breath away. "I heard Harris mention the mummy unwrapping party."

Harris, I surmised was the butler who had opened the door.

"Yes, Lady Ashmoore," Lestrade said, "We came to ask

your husband about the party and those who attended it."

Lady Ashmoore seated herself, spreading her skirts around her carefully. She obviously intended to stay for the discussion. I saw my friend watching her carefully, with no little interest. It was unlike him to take an interest in the fair sex.

"It was mostly the men who attended the actual unwrapping," Lady Ashmoore said.

"The men?" I asked.

Holmes's tone was amused, "Well-bred ladies, my dear Watson, do not look upon the naked bodies of men; no matter how long they have been dead."

"Ah. Of course. My apologies, Lady Ashmoore, I did not think."

The lady waved off my apology with a smile. "I am afraid I do not yet know all of my husband's friends well." She turned to the man in question. "Do you remember who was here?"

Lord Ashmoore shrugged. "The usual. Collins will still have the list."

"The list?" Lestrade asked.

"The invitation list," Lord Ashmoore explained.

"If we could speak with Collins, I would be obliged," Lestrade said.

"Of course," Lord Ashmoore replied. He rang for the

butler who speedily arrived and was despatched to fetch the man Collins. "Tell him to bring the guest list from the unwrapping," Lord Ashmoore barked at his butler's retreating back.

A few minutes later a short, bespectacled man, with the demeanour of an anxious ferret, fairly scuttled into the room. "You wished to see me, m'lord?"

Lord Ashmoore gave him an irritated look. "I sent for you, did I not?"

"Yes, m'lord," came the whispered reply.

"The detectives wish to know who was at the mummy unwrapping. Kindly tell them."

The man, Collins, looked down at the sheet of paper in his hand. "There was Lord Francis Harkness and his wife, Lady Constance," his voice was still a whisper.

Holmes held his hand out to Collins. "If I may?"

Collins hand the paper to Holmes without a word.

Holmes read aloud in a strong voice, "Lord Sebastian Clavering, the Hon. Phillip Ashmoore..." He looked at Lord Ashmoore in silent query.

"My cousin," His Lordship replied.

"Mr Albert Granger, M.P. and his wife and daughter."

"Unusual to include the daughter," Lestrade commented.

"She is engaged to my cousin," Lord Ashmoore replied.

"And finally, a Mr. and Mrs. Robert Wilson."

The last two names seemed a little unusual for a titled gathering. Lord Ashmoore understood my unspoken question. "Wilson is a banker. Helped finance the expedition. It was only polite to include him." Lord Ashmoore's tone told me that he would really rather not have been polite.

"I believe an actor was present to recite the curse?" Holmes said.

Lord Ashmoore sniffed. "He was not a guest."

"Nevertheless, we shall need his name and address," Lestrade said. "As we shall need the addresses of the actual guests."

"Why are detectives interested in Reginald's little party?" Lady Ashmoore asked, her eyes alight with curiosity.

"The doctor and his assistants who did the unwrapping have been murdered, my lady," Lestrade said.

Lady Ashmoore put her hand to her mouth in shock. "Oh no! How dreadful!" She turned to her husband. "Reginald, you must do all that you can to assist."

Lord Ashmoore patted his wife's hand gently. "Do not worry your pretty head, Veronica. All will be taken care of." He turned to his secretary, "Collins, give the gentlemen the information they require."

Then he turned back to us. "I trust there is nothing else I can do for you?" His tone suggested that he would prefer it.

Holmes inclined his head. "Not at this time, Lord Ashmoore. We may need to speak with you again."

"Very well," Ashmoore's tone was grudging. "But next time, kindly make an appointment!"

"With all due respect, Lord Ashmoore, a constable was sent around yesterday to advise you of our coming," Lestrade replied, his tone curt.

Lord Ashmoore made a grumbling noise and placed his arm around his wife and led her from the room. Holmes watched them go with an expression of intense curiosity on his face.

Collins muttered something about fetching the addresses for us and scuttled from the room in his master's wake. It was the butler who returned shortly afterwards and handed Lestrade a list of the names and addresses of the attendees and then politely escorted us to the door.

Outside the house, Lestrade blew out a sharp breath. "Whew! What an unpleasant chap!"

"Indeed," Holmes responded, his thoughts clearly elsewhere.

"I see you were captivated by Lady Ashmoore's beauty," I commented with a sly smile.

Holmes shook his head. "Not at all, Watson. I do not doubt that Lady Ashmoore is considered a great beauty by society, but that is not what intrigues me about the lady."

"What is it that does?" Lestrade asked.

"Why does a woman of obvious intelligence take such pains to portray herself as one with brains full of dandelion fluff?"

"Obvious intelligence?" I asked.

It was Holmes's turn to smile slyly. "You were so taken by her beauty, my friend that you failed to notice anything else."

"Such as?"

"The light of intelligent curiosity in her eyes. It is one thing that is hard to hide."

Lestrade shrugged. "A lot of men don't care for intelligent women, Holmes. The lady most likely takes care not to seem too intelligent in front of her husband. Lord Ashmoore strikes me as the sort who would not take well to his wife being more intelligent than him."

"Perhaps," Holmes murmured. "Or perhaps not. Time will tell. Let us look at these addresses, Lestrade, and work out our order of visits."

Chapter Eight

The first address on the list was that for Lord Francis Harkness. His lordship lived across the Thames in Richmond. We crossed the river over the Richmond Bridge, a fine stone arch bridge that had been completed in 1777. The view along the Thames was charming, and I gazed happily out of the cab window as we crossed.

Upon hearing our names when we arrived at the house, which would be better described as a mansion, the liveried butler immediately showed us into a luxurious parlour.

Lestrade and I exchanged puzzled looks. This was not the reception that either of us had been expecting. Holmes just smiled slightly at our bewilderment. It was obvious that he knew the reason for our reception.

A few minutes later a young handsome man of middling height, with blonde hair and blue eyes entered the room. There was something familiar about him that I could not place. He was accompanied by a woman of similar age, who was plump and pretty in a fashion best described as vapid. The man came straight to Holmes and held out his hand. "Mr. Holmes, it is a pleasure to meet you. I have never had the chance to thank you for what you did for my cousin."

"The pleasure is mine, Lord Francis. How is Sir Lucas?"

"Luci is well. Aunt Amelia writes that he has found a

companion. A young man who aspires to be a writer. She tells me that he is a charming lad who adores Luci."

I realized then that our host was a relative of Sir Lucas Catterick, 5th Baronet Undershaw, whose secretary and companion Thomas Arbuthnot had been murdered several years ago. It was a case that had ended in a terrifying encounter on Westminster Bridge that almost cost me my life.

Lord Francis turned to Lestrade and me and shook both our hands. He gave me a sad smile. "I am sure you will be saddened to learn, Doctor, that my grandmother, Lady Caroline Harkness, recently passed away."

"I am sorry to hear this, Lord Francis. Lady Caroline was a charming and formidable lady."

"She derived a great deal of pleasure in having met you."

"And I her. I am only sorry that I was never able to tell her stories of Holmes's adventures as I promised."

"France is a little far to go to entertain an old lady with stories," Lord Francis said with a smile.

"If there is a charming lady and tea involved," Holmes said drily, "My good Watson would go twice as far."

Lord Francis's companion laughed lightly at this. The man turned to her with a smile. "Pray forgive me, I have not introduced you." Lord Francis turned back to us. "Gentlemen, this is my wife, Lady Constance Harkness."

"A pleasure to meet you, m'lady," Lestrade said. Holmes and I echoed the sentiment.

Lord Francis gestured for us all to be seated. Once we had done so, he said, "Now, I am curious to learn the reason for your visit."

"The reason is Lord Ashmoore's mummy unwrapping party, and the subsequent murder of the doctor who performed it and both of his assistants," Lestrade replied.

Lord Francis looked astounded. "Good god!"

Lady Constance clasped a hand to her mouth in horror.

Lord Francis looked at his wife. "Any help we can give, we will do so."

"What do you remember of the night? Does anything stand out?" asked Holmes. "I do realize that it was several weeks ago."

"It was a crushing bore, to be honest," Lord Francis replied. "Ashmoore was a friend of my father's. Lady Veronica is his second wife. Part of the reason for the mummy unwrapping was for his wife to make some acceptable acquaintances."

"Not that he invited many people that society would deem acceptable," Lady Constance commented. "Though Cecelia Granger, the wife of that Member of Parliament is well-liked."

Holmes caught what was not being said. "But other attendees less so? Were you thinking of anyone in particular?"

Lady Constance sighed. "Mrs. Wilson. The wife of the banker who helped finance the expedition. She had no idea of what is expected of a lady in social situations."

"What do you mean?" I asked.

"When Lady Veronica, Mrs. and Miss Granger and I retired when the unwrapping began, Mrs. Wilson insisted on remaining with the men to see the fun."

"Not the done thing at all," Lord Francis observed.

"When did you retire?" Lestrade asked.

Lady Constance gave a slight shiver. "After the actor, Jeremy Blanding, read the curse aloud. To be honest, I was glad to get out of the room."

"I wish I could have," Lord Francis said. "It was really quite boring. I was expecting to learn something; however, all Ashmoore was interested in was getting the bandages off the mummy with speed and getting his hands on whatever items were concealed in them."

"What about the others who attended?" Holmes asked.

"Clavering was as bored as I was, and not afraid to show it."

"That would be Lord Sebastian Clavering?" Lestrade asked, consulting his notes.

Lord Francis nodded. "He lives quite close by here in Richmond. Bas is a pleasant fellow. I assume that you will be going to see him?

Holmes nodded. "Once we take our leave of you. The other two couples, as well as Lord Ashmoore's cousin, all live closer in."

"I am not sure if we can really tell you anything else," Lord Francis said. "Constance did not view the unwrapping and I was bored by it. I avoided the banker, Wilson; he kept trying to persuade me to switch my accounts to his bank. Very bad form, that. And I do not know Granger well enough to talk informally with him."

Holmes got to his feet. Lestrade and I followed him. "Thank you for your time, Lord Francis, Lady Constance."

"It was our please, gentlemen," Lord Francis replied, holding out his hand for us all to shake once more.

We took our leave from the couple and then headed off to the home of Lord Sebastian Clavering.

Clavering House was a sprawling Elizabethan affair with grounds that sloped down to the Thames. A poker-faced butler met us at the door and escorted us out into the grounds at the rear of the building.

Amongst the outbuildings I could see what appeared to be an enormous glass house, as well as several aviaries.

We stood waiting whilst a footman was sent to find Lord Clavering. Eventually he returned trailing behind a tall man, with black curly hair, wearing an eyepatch over his left eye, from under which several scars protruded. It gave the man a raffish air that was offset by his broad smile of welcome as he approached us.

"Gentlemen, what can I do for you? Thompson tells me that you are from Scotland Yard." He indicated the footman trailing behind him.

"I am from Scotland Yar, m'lord," Lestrade said. "Inspector Lestrade, at your service. These gentlemen are Mr. Sherlock Holmes and Dr. John Watson. We wish to speak to you about Lord Ashmoore's mummy unwrapping."

Clavering snorted. "Old Reggie and his mouldering mummies. The man's half mad, you know. Come, let me show you around and we can talk."

He turned and began to walk away, leaving us to follow. "I fail to see what interest Reggie's mummy would have for Scotland Yard."

"The mummy unwrapping itself, very little," Holmes replied. "The murders that followed in its wake, however, are interesting indeed."

Clavering stopped and turned to stare at us, his one remaining eye blinking furiously. "Murders?"

"Those of Dr. Simpson and his two assistants," Lestrade said.

"Killed in the manner described in the curse," I added.

Clavering stared at us. "Good Lord! It is like something out of a penny dreadful! Not that I read those things, of course."

I found my eyes drifting towards the eye patch as Lord Clavering talked. Lord Clavering saw my look. "Professional interest, doctor?"

"Very much so," I replied. "One rarely sees ocular damage to such an extent."

"Not damage," Holmes observed, "…but destruction. Those scars…"

Lord Clavering nodded and touched the patch gently, seemingly unaffected by our curiosity. "Legacy of a run-in with Priscilla."

I wondered who on earth Priscilla was. Surely not his wife. His mistress, perhaps.

"Did you report the lady to the police?" Lestrade asked.

Clavering chuckled. "Oh, Priscilla is most definitely *not* a lady. Come, you must meet her."

The three of us exchanged puzzled looks before following Clavering to one of the largest out-buildings. I took it to be some kind of storage shed, excepting that it had large windows that looked out over the grounds. Clavering unlocked the door and disappeared inside cooing, "Priscilla, my sweet, come and meet my new acquaintances."

I was, frankly, horrified. Lord Clavering was obviously keeping a woman prisoner. No wonder she had attacked him! Lestrade looked as horrified as I was. Holmes merely looked amused.

A few moments later, Lord Clavering come out of the door with a sturdy leather lead in his hand. On the end of it stood a half-grown white tiger!

Holmes laughed delightedly. "A tiger! I thought perhaps a cheetah, as I believe they are easier to obtain."

"Holmes, what on earth do you mean?" I asked.

"Lord Clavering's scars, my dear Watson, were obviously caused by the claws of some great cat. As I said, I thought a cheetah to be the most likely culprit."

Lord Clavering looked down proudly at the elegant creature. "She is a beauty, is she not? I got her from Jamrach's Animal Emporium. They are helping me stock my menagerie. It is rather small at the moment, but it will grow. Rather like Priscilla, here."

He took the tiger back inside its enclosure then rejoined us outside. "Now, let us walk and I will answer your questions."

"Forgive me the impertinence, Lord Clavering," Lestrade said, "…but it seems to me that your interests and Lord Ashmoore's do not exactly coincide…"

"And you are wondering why he invited me to the party?"

"Frankly, yes."

"He thought I might be interested because of one of my animals."

Lord Clavering led us to the large greenhouse I had spotted earlier. He unlocked the door and led us inside. The greenhouse did not hold many plants. The centrepiece was a large, seemingly deep, pool of water, with iron railing around it.

Two beady eyes peered out of the water at us.

"Gentlemen, meet Sobek. He is a juvenile Nile River crocodile. Lord Ashmoore brought his wife out to view my animals. When he heard this fellow's name, he invited me to the unwrapping."

"His name?" I asked, somewhat confused.

"As I said this fine fellow is Sobek. Sobek, or Sebek, was the Egyptian crocodile-headed god. He was associated with the power of the pharaoh, as well as fertility and military prowess. His cultic centre was at the aptly named Crocodilopolis on Lake Moeris."

"So, when Lord Ashmoore heard the name, he assumed you were as interested in ancient Egypt as he is," said Lestrade.

"Exactly, Inspector. I really could not turn down the invitation without seeming rude." Lord Clavering looked between the two of us. "...and to be honest, gentlemen, I felt that the mummy unwrapping would most likely be the least boring of any other function that Ashmoore would invite me to in return."

Holmes had wandered away from us and was looking around the place with a great deal of curiosity. He came back carrying a large ball of heavy twine. "This is excellent rope, Your Lordship. May I be so bold as to take a sample of it?"

Lord Clavering gave him a bewildered look. "Please, help yourself, Mr. Holmes."

"Thank you." Holmes took a knife from his pocket and

carefully cut off about of foot of rope, which he then stored safely away in his pocket.

We took our leave of His Lordship and walked back out to where the cab was waiting.

"Rope, Holmes?" I asked. "What on earth...?"

"If I am not mistaken, my dear Watson, this rope is the same as that used to tie all three of the victims."

"Are you certain?" Lestrade demanded.

"As certain as I can be until I compare this sample to the one that I took from the mortuary."

Lestrade looked back at Clavering House. "Could His Lordship be the killer?"

"It is far too early to speculate, Lestrade," Holmes said in mild reproof.

"Lord Sebastian Clavering is not even interested in ancient Egypt," I pointed out.

Lestrade snorted at that. "I would point out that the man has named his pet crocodile after an Egyptian god and knows rather a lot about said god for a man who claims to have no interest in the subject."

"Well spotted, Lestrade," Holmes congratulated him. "But knowledge does not equal motive."

"So, you do not consider him a suspect?" Lestrade challenged.

"I did not say that," replied Holmes, his tone holding

mild reproof. "We do not have enough pieces of the puzzle to even begin to put together a picture of our killers." He climbed into the waiting cab. "I do believe it is time that we called upon the next people on our list."

"And that would be?" I asked.

"Lestrade looked at his notebook. "The banker, Robert Wilson, and his wife."

Chapter Nine

The Wilsons lived in a smart townhouse close to Kensington Gardens. Mr. Wilson was not at home, but his wife dispatched a servant to his place of work to fetch him when she heard the reason for our visit.

We waited perhaps an hour, drinking tea, and making abysmal small talk with Mrs. Wilson, before the opening of the front door heralded the return of Mr. Wilson.

We rose to our feet as the man entered the room. Robert Wilson was a short man, with a dour expression, and an air of pomposity.

"Thank you for coming home, sir," Lestrade said after he had introduced us. "It was not necessary. We could have come to your place of work."

"It is of no matter, Inspector. I own the bank, so I may take time off as I wish. Naturally, when I heard that the great Sherlock Holmes and his friend Doctor Watson, not to mention your august self, were at my house, well, I just had to return home."

We all sat down. Mrs. Wilson sent for a fresh pot of tea for her husband.

"You own a bank, you said?" Lestrade asked.

"I do. Wilson and Son Commercial Bank. My father started it. We are not a large bank, dealing as we do mostly with small businesses, but I have hopes for expansion."

"Is that why you helped finance Lord Ashmoore's Egypt

expedition?" asked Holmes.

"It is. I thought it worth the risk, for the possibility of bringing old money into the fold. I had hoped that the mummy unwrapping would allow me to make valuable contacts."

I caught the downcast note to his voice. "But it did not?"

"No, Doctor Watson, it did not. I was virtually snubbed by everyone except Lord Ashmoore himself."

I personally thought that the only reason for that is that His Lordship would want to keep the banker sweet to assist with financing future expeditions.

Wilson was unable to add anything to our knowledge, except the realization that the reason for his being snubbed was not so much his profession, as his wife.

The woman simpered and giggled about the unwrapping. "It was ever so funny to see. A man all shrivelled up and shiny like a piece of furniture." Her voice dropped to what she obviously believed was a saucy whisper. "They had tied his penis to his leg, would you believe? I asked the archaeologist gentleman why they did that. Apparently, it was to stop it falling off when the corpse dried out. Isn't that the most fascinating thing you have ever heard?"

As I struggled for an answer, Holmes got to his feet. Lestrade and I hastily followed.

"Thank you for your time, Mr. Wilson, Mrs. Wilson. You have been most helpful," Holmes said. We took our leave with Mrs. Wilson's exhortations to do call again ringing in our ears.

"I would rather spend the next six months patrolling Whitechapel, at night, alone than spend any more time with that woman," Lestrade muttered once we were safely outside and out of earshot. "Where to now, Holmes?"

Holmes consulted his fob watch. "I believe the Grangers live close to here. We should still have time to see them, and perhaps Phillip Ashmoore, today. We may have to leave Jeremy Blanding until tomorrow."

The Grangers lived only a short walk from the Wilsons' house, so we dismissed the cab and walked. We would summon another cab to take us to Phillip Ashmoore's home.

As it happened, that proved to be unnecessary as Phillip Ashmoore was visiting his fiancée and her parents when we arrived.

The Grangers were a solidly middle-class couple, who invited us in quite civilly when we arrived on their doorstep. Albert Granger, M.P., was of middling height, with a corporation not unlike that of Mycroft Holmes. His dark brown hair was thinning, and his sharp blue eyes looked out at us from behind gold-rimmed spectacles. Mrs. Cecelia Granger was of a height with her husband, with soft, blonde hair held back firmly in a respectable bun, and soft grey eyes that greeted us warmly.

We were escorted into a well-appointed parlour where a

young woman, whose resemblance to the couple showed her to be their daughter, Davina, and a young man who rose to his feet as we entered.

"Inspector Lestrade, Mr. Holmes, Doctor Watson, it is a pleasure to meet you. My cousin said you may be calling."

"You must be Mr. Phillip Ashmoore, then," Holmes said.

"I am, sir."

I own that I was a little surprised. When Lord Ashmoore had said that his cousin had attended, I had expected him to be older, perhaps closer in age to His Lordship. My surprise must have shown on my face, as the young man laughed. "You were expecting someone older, Doctor Watson."

"I was," I admitted.

"It is actually my father who is Lord Ashmoore's cousin, their fathers being brothers. Cousin is simpler than trying to work out exactly how we are related."

Lestrade smiled. "We do something similar in my own family," he said.

"It is simpler in the long run, don't you think, Inspector?"

"Indeed, it is, Mr. Ashmoore."

"We were discussing the party when you gentlemen arrived," Albert Granger said. "None of us can think of anything untoward occurring that may have led to these dreadful murders."

Phillip Ashmoore nodded in agreement. "It was quite a dull affair, if one is honest."

"Except for the actor reciting the curse," Davina Granger said. "That was quite thrilling."

"True," Phillip Ashmoore agreed. "Blanding is known for his sepulchral tones. We saw him in as the vampire Sir Alan Raby in a revival of Dion Boucicault's play *The Vampire*. I did mention how good he was in the role to Reggie, which may have been why he hired him to read the curse."

Holmes nodded and got to his feet. Lestrade and I followed. "Thank you for taking the time to see us."

"Not at all, gentlemen," Albert Granger replied, rising to his feet to show us to the door.

Once outside I said to Holmes, "That was rather a short visit."

Holmes shrugged. "I fear there is nothing to learn there. You heard Granger. They have been discussing it."

"You mean they have had time to get their stories to line up?" queried Lestrade.

"Exactly. Speaking to them now is a waste of our time. Oh well, at least we will have time to speak with Mr. Blanding today after all."

"And then Mycroft?" I asked.

"And then Mycroft," Holmes confirmed.

Jeremy Blanding lived in Marylebone, quite close to Baker Street, but not in accommodations as fine as that provided by Mrs. Hudson.

Blanding's landlady was a sour-faced woman who let us in grudgingly, before showing us to her tenant's door.

Jeremy Blanding opened the door upon our knock, yawning widely. He looked dishevelled and half asleep. When we introduced ourselves, he nodded and said, "Pray forgive me, gentlemen, I have only just risen."

"You are currently working?" Holmes asked.

Blanding nodded again, opening the door wider to let us in. "I'm playing Tom Hatchet in Douglas Jerrold's *Black-Eyed Susan* at the Surrey in Southwark. George Conquest, that's the manager, does like melodramas. He's written a few himself. They're good for getting an audience in."

"We are here about the little performance you put on for Lord Reginald Ashmoore," Lestrade said.

Blanding stifled another yawn and rang the bell for his landlady to bring him coffee. He waited until that good lady had departed before pouring himself a cup and offering it to us. We all declined.

"A little too late in the day for me," Lestrade said.

"That I can understand," said Blanding. "However, if I don't drink it I would no doubt fall asleep on stage." He took a large sip of the beverage. "What do you wish to know about the

Ashmoore party? It seems a strange thing to bring detectives to my door."

"Have you seen the newspapers at all, Mr. Blanding?" Holmes asked.

Blanding shook his head. "Unless it is theatre reviews, I don't bother with them."

"Then you will not have heard that three men have been murdered in the same manner as the charmingly specific curse that you read aloud at the party," Lestrade said.

Blanding put his coffee cup down and stared at us. "Good Lord! Who has been murdered and why?"

"The doctor who did the unwrapping and his two assistants," I said.

"As to why, as yet we have no motive for the crimes," Holmes added. "Why did Lord Ashmoore select you to do the reading?" Phillip Ashmoore had already told us, but I suspected Holmes wished to hear it from Blanding.

"Some cousin of His Lordship had seen me in another play. Told him he thought I would do an excellent job. Lord Ashmoore tracked me down, offered me six sovereigns and a meal to do the job." He pulled a face. "The meal was in the kitchen with the servants, not the guests, but the money was welcome. Ashmoore isn't mean with his servants' food either. We had calf's head soup, followed by a tasty eel pie, and barberry tart with clotted cream. In my profession it is either a feast or a famine, so the meal was most definitely welcome."

Blanding frowned. "After I had eaten. I went up to what I think was the billiard room. The mummy was laid out on a table covered with a cloth. The lights were dimmed, I recited the curse in a suitable voice, then I slipped out and came home."

"Did you recognise any of the guests?" Lestrade asked.

Blanding shook his head. "No. I do not frequent those social circles. Not like Sir Henry Irving and his ilk."

We thanked Jeremy Blanding for his time and took our leave. Outside, Holmes once again consulted his fob watch, then turned to hail a cab. "Time to head to the Diogenes Club and see what light my brother can shed on the dramatis personae of this case."

Chapter Ten

Mycroft Holmes seemed pleased to see us when we were ushered into the Stranger's Room at the Diogenes Club. With his regular round of rooms, office, and club, I supposed that it was unlikely that Mycroft saw many people. A visit from his brother would mean a new and interesting puzzle – marking a difference from the usual sorting of information that made Mycroft so indispensable to both Her Majesty and Her Majesty's government.

"Sherlock! What brings you here? With the good doctor and Inspector Lestrade, no less." He held up a hand. "No, do not tell me. It is the murders of Dr. Simpson and his assistants."

Mycroft's swift comprehension always astounded me. He must have seen the look on my face and chuckled. "Those murders are the only ones currently being handled by Scotland Yard that qualify as unusual enough to get my brother involved."

"Quite," Holmes said, as he took a seat close to his brother. Lestrade and I both found seats and settled in.

Mycroft poured us all a brandy, before settling back into his chair. "Now, tell me exactly what brings you to me, Sherlock?"

"Information, Mycroft. On three people."

"And those people are?"

"Abasi Tarek, Lord Sebastian Clavering, and Lady

Veronica Ashmoore."

Both Lestrade and I raised our eyebrows at the lady being included on the list.

Mycroft took a sip of his brandy. "You consider them suspects?"

Holmes shook his head. "I consider no one a suspect, at the moment. Those three people are ones that I have minimal information on, and I would like more."

Mycroft nodded thoughtfully. "Abasi Tarek is the Khedive of Egypt's agent in London, as I am sure you are aware."

"He said that he mostly organizes imports to and exports from Egypt and occasionally undertakes other commissions for the Khedive," Holmes said.

"Such as finding out what happened to the relics from the tomb of Neb-Heka-Ra," I added.

Mycroft nodded again. "He does all that. We suspect he is also trying to find out the government's plans for his country."

"Plans?" I asked.

"Egypt is a British Protectorate, of a sort," Mycroft replied. "The Egyptian army is led by Kitchener, and Sir Evelyn Baring is Controller-General. The Khedive might outwardly support them, but he is known to resent their presence."

"As well he might," Holmes added.

"The Khedive has nationalist leanings and links with the Ottoman Empire," Mycroft continued.

"Does this Abasi Tarek?" Lestrade asked.

Mycroft shook his head. "That we do not know conclusively. It is most likely. The Khedive is unlikely to have sent someone known to be pro-British into what is effectively a spying role."

"You have tried to subvert him," Holmes stated.

"Let us just say that Tarek is an honest man who is not open to bribery of any sort."

"Anything else?" Lestrade asked.

Mycroft shook his head. "His office is on the Strand, something I am also sure you already know. He lives in several rooms above his office. Tarek only goes out for meals, the occasional walk along the Thames, and to send reports back to Egypt."

"Reports which you read before they are sent," Holmes observed.

"Of course," Mycroft returned mildly.

"What of Lord Clavering?" Holmes asked.

"Not political and unlikely to be a murderer. Unless someone killed one of his animals," Mycroft replied. "The Clavering family started in trade. Lord Sebastian's great-grandfather was given a knighthood. He bought land on the

Thames at Richmond and kept adding to it as other people sold. The estate is now extremely large. His grandfather was given a title for services to the crown when King George IV took the throne."

Holmes snorted. "You mean he loaned money to Prinny who could not pay him back, so gave him a title in consolation."

"Those are, essentially, the facts."

King George IV, who had been known as Prinny when he was Prince Regent for his father King George III, had been a wastrel who spent enormous amounts of money on gluttony, clothing, and architecture. When he became king, his ministers considered him selfish and irresponsible. The people loathed him for the way he treated his wife, Caroline of Brunswick. His locking her out of his coronation had caused a monumental scandal.

"And Lady Veronica?" Holmes asked.

Mycroft frowned and put his brandy down. "I cannot help you with Lady Veronica Ashmoore."

"Cannot, or will not?"

"Cannot," Mycroft admitted. "I know nothing about her. My people cannot find anything about her. Lord Reginald married her when he was on the Continent. We do not even know where they met. Any information you can give me would be more than I had previously."

"Interesting," Holmes commented, getting to his feet. "Thank you for your time, Mycroft."

"It was a pleasure, Sherlock. Please do let me know how the case progresses. And if you need any assistance."

Lestrade and I followed Holmes out of the Diogenes Club, where Lestrade took his leave from us. Holmes and I flagged down a cab and returned to Baker Street for a well-earned dinner.

Mrs. Hudson had anticipated us returning hungry and served up a delicious meal of creamy cucumber soup, followed by baked carp with vegetable marrow in white sauce, finished with a tasty baked apple pudding.

I concluded the evening with a glass of whisky while I read *The Nether World* by George Gissing. It made for bleak, though entertaining, reading. Being a novel of London's poor.

Holmes was brooding in his chair with a pipe of tobacco. He was still sitting there like some form of statue, or more accurately, a gargoyle, when I went to bed.

Holmes and I were eating a hearty breakfast of poached eggs, black pudding, and baked mushrooms, washed down with coffee, when Lestrade came pounding on our door.

He almost fell into the room when I opened the door.

Holmes observed the inspector for a moment. "From your agitation I assume there has been another murder?"

"There has," Lestrade replied. "One of Lord Sebastian

Clavering's footmen came to the Yard. Lord Clavering found a body in one of his outbuildings not two hours ago. His lordship sent for me."

"No doubt assuming that it must be connected to our visit yesterday," I commented.

Holmes frowned. "Perhaps, or perhaps not. Much will depend on the identity of the corpse."

"But it has to be connected,' Lestrade said. "We visit a man and then a corpse turns up on his property the very next day."

"It is never wise, Lestrade, to theorize before you have all the facts," Holmes admonished him.

Holmes rose to his feet, placing his napkin beside his plate. I did the same. We fetched our coats and hats and followed Lestrade down to Baker Street, where a police growler sat patiently at the kerb.

The driver set a brisk pace towards Richmond. There was no chatter. It was clear that Holmes was in no mood for it, so I occupied myself looking out the window at the people and buildings. London, for all its dirt and, at times, outright squalor, is a beautiful city, and well worth looking at.

A footman was waiting for us at the gates to Clavering House. He showed the police driver where to park and led Holmes, Lestrade and me round the back. I saw that we were headed for the greenhouse that housed Sobek, Lord Clavering's juvenile Nile crocodile.

Lord Clavering was sitting in a chair that had been placed directly in front of the door. He looked vaguely ill, as if he had been drinking all night. Clavering looked up as we approached. I realized then that I was wrong. The haunted, sickened, look in the man's eyes told me that excess alcohol was not the cause of his pallor, but the sight of something dreadful that was beyond his experience.

Relief flooded his face at the sight of us and he got to his feet. "Thank God you have come. It is ghastly."

Lestrade's voice was soothing. "I am sure it was m'lord. Where is the corpse?"

"In there," Lord Clavering pointed at the greenhouse.

He unlocked the greenhouse door and gestured for us to enter ahead of him. I could see that he was not keen to be returning, but obviously felt that he was obliged to.

Sobek, I noticed, appeared to be sulking down one end of his pool. A pile of what appeared to be joints of meat sat in an untidy heap near the door, with two burly footmen standing guard over it; their eyes never leaving Sobek, who splashed his tail in annoyance.

It took me a moment to realize that what I had taken to be joints of meat was actually a dismembered human body.

Lord Clavering gestured at the pile, keeping his eyes averted. "I came in here to feed Sobek and found those floating in the pool. I did not realize what they were at first. I got a net and began to fish them out. I fished the head out first. I could not believe what I was seeing. I thought it was someone's idea of a joke. Then the tongue lolled out of the head."

Lord Clavering began to shake violently. I sent one of the footmen to bring the chair in and dispatched the other for brandy and a blanket. It was obvious that the man was going into shock.

Holmes went over to examine the gruesome pile. He fished around for a moment and came up with the head. "Hmmm, you were correct, Lestrade. This is connected to our case."

"How do you know?" I asked, not looking at Holmes or what he was holding. I had seen some horrific things when I was in Afghanistan, but this was almost worse than anything I had seen there.

Holmes turned towards us, still holding the head. He raised it towards us. Reluctantly, I turned to look. Lestrade took a step forward, a frown on his face.

"Is that..."

"Mr. Joseph Brown. Secretary to the archaeologist Mr. Bernard Barrett." Holmes frowned. "Even though Brown was not at the unwrapping, someone knew he was connected to the excavation of the tomb."

Lestrade immediately sent another of the footmen for the local doctor. When he arrived, he took one look at the body and hurriedly agreed with Lestrade that it would be best if Dr. Bond handled the case, seeing as that gentleman had much more experience with such things.

"The most I ever see, gentlemen, are drownings," he informed us, before rapidly vacating the greenhouse, to be plied with some of Lord Clavering's brandy, before heading on his way.

The footman who had gone for the doctor was then dispatched to the City in the police growler to bring Dr. Bond to the scene.

Holmes continued to examine the corpse. "Well, I think we can safely say that we now know what happened to Dr. Simpson's missing bone saw. Look at this."

Holmes thrust an arm under my nose. "As you can see, the bone is cut through cleanly, if a little unprofessionally."

I examined the arm and found myself in agreement with my friend.

Lord Clavering, meanwhile, was still huddled in the chair with a blanket wrapped around him. He was staring at a corner of the greenhouse with a frown on his face.

Lestrade gave me a worried look. "Is Lord Clavering all right?" he asked me in a whisper.

"He is in shock, Lestrade. It takes people differently," I replied, as I walked over to his lordship. "How are you feeling now, my lord?" I asked softly.

"It has gone," he replied, looking up at me with a puzzled expression.

"What has gone?" I asked.

"The rope. Someone has stolen a whole ball of rope."

I was beginning to wonder if the ordeal had scattered the man's wits when Holmes spoke up.

"Indeed, it has, Lord Clavering. There was a ball of rope sitting in that corner yesterday. I took a sample of it." He looked closely at the man. "Why don't you go into the house and rest."

"I have to feed Sobek," Lord Clavering objected.

"There is food for him here?"

Lord Clavering pointed to a bucket full of fish sitting just inside the door.

"We will feed him, my lord. I think you should go and rest. Do you not agree, *Doctor* Watson?"

I felt that Holmes emphasised my title to get through to the man. "Absolutely. Rest is the best cure for shock." I gestured to the remaining footman, who came and gently led Lord Clavering away.

Lestrade watched him go. "The was odd. Fixated on a ball of rope. Do I need to add the crime of theft to the list of charges when we catch the culprits?"

I frowned. "It is not common, but such fixations can be a reaction to severe shock. The mind looks for something else to focus on. In this instance, Lord Clavering noticed that something that should have been in its place was not. His mind latched on to that to avoid thinking about what he had seen earlier."

Lestrade shuddered. "I can understand that. I really do not want to think about what has happened, and I am an experienced police officer."

While we waited for Dr. Bond to arrive, Lestrade and I threw fish to Sobek. The creature was obviously pleased at finally being fed.

Holmes prowled the greenhouse examining everything, even going outside to examine the door. He came back in wearing a disgruntled expression. "The lock on the door is a simple one. A child could pick it."

"To be fair, Holmes, there isn't much in here to steal," Lestrade said.

"Except for the ball of rope," I added. "Whilst someone might want to steal the crocodile, I rather think the noise the attempt would make would get them caught."

Holmes was looking at the crocodile, an odd expression on his face. I heard him murmur "May the Crocodile of Sobek rend his flesh."

Lestrade swore. "That damned curse."

"It narrows the suspect list at least," Holmes commented.

"What do you mean?" I asked.

"Before, we had to ask who knew about the curse. Now,

the question is, who knew about the crocodile," Holmes replied.

Dr. Bond arrived in a plain black landau that greatly resembled a hearse. Two mortuary attendants accompanied him. The doctor listened gravely as Lestrade outlined what had occurred in the greenhouse, before going over to the pile of remains and examining them as his assistants carefully placed them in two large canvas sacks.

He came back to where we were standing with a frown on his face. "Given the dismemberment of the body, I am unlikely to be able to give you a cause of death."

Lestrade sighed. "I was afraid that would be the case."

"I can tell you one thing, however."

"And that is?" Holmes asked.

"The crocodile has not developed a taste for human flesh. There are no bite marks on any of the body parts that I can see." Dr. Bond looked at Sobek, who had gone back to sulking at the far end of his pool, once it had become obvious that no more fish would be forthcoming. "I think that will come as something of a relief to the owner."

I thought about it for a moment and agreed with Dr. Bond. Telling Lord Clavering that his pet had to be destroyed could have done incalculable damage to the man's mind in his current state.

We waited until Dr. Bond and his men had left with their grisly burden. Then we went up to the house. The butler met us at the door.

Holmes looked at the man, "Please tell his Lord Clavering that the remains have been removed, Sobek and been fed, and that there is no sign that Sobek attempted to eat what was thrown into his pool. When Lord Clavering has recovered, please ask him who amongst the guests at Lord Ashmoore's party knew about Sobek. Have someone bring his response to me at Baker Street."

The butler nodded. "I will do so, Mr. Holmes."

We took our leave and the journey back into London proper took place in a subdued manner. Holmes was lost in thought, and I was still dealing with the horror of what we had seen. Lestrade was also sunk deep into silence. We were perhaps halfway home when Holmes roused himself from his thoughts.

"Lestrade, instruct the driver that we need to make another visit."

"To whom, Holmes?" Lestrade asked.

"Mr. Bernard Barrett. He needs to know what has happened. And in light of what Abasi Tarek told us, he has more than a few questions to answer."

Chapter Eleven

The growler took us to the flat we had visited just a few days before.

Barrett's angry visage melted away into a more amiable expression when he opened the door to our sharp knocks.

"Forgive me gentlemen, I was working. Brown should be here. I have no idea where he has got to."

"As it happens, Mr. Barrett," Lestrade said. "We know exactly where he is. May we come in?"

Barrett stood back and allowed us to enter the rooms. "Where is Brown?" Barrett asked. "He went out last evening and did not return."

"Were you not surprised that he did not return?" Holmes asked.

Barrett shrugged. "Brown is a grown man. He works for me as secretary when I am in London and as my foreman of works when I am on a dig. If he wishes a night for himself with some whore, who am I to tell him no?"

"Does he frequent whores a lot?" Lestrade asked.

Barrett shrugged again. "Not often. He has urges, like most men. With the life we both lead, a whore is a better option than a wife." He looked closely as us. "Has something happened? Has he been robbed or something?"

Lestrade looked at the man. "You had best sit down, Mr. Barrett."

Barrett looked at our faces, then dropped into a nearby chair. "What has happened?"

"There is no easy way to say this," Lestrade said. "The remains of Mr. Joseph Brown were found this morning."

"Remains?" Barrett started to pale.

"Mr. Brown was killed in a manner yet to be determined," Lestrade said softly. "He was then dismembered, and his remains left at the manor of Lord Sebastian Clavering. In the enclosure of Lord Clavering's pet Nile crocodile, to be exact."

Barrett looked at us in horror, then dropped his face into his hands. "The curse!"

"May the Crocodile of Sobek rend his flesh," Holmes said softly.

"That part, at least, did not happen," Lestrade said. "Dr. Bond assures us that Lord Clavering's pet, also named Sobek, did not so much as nip the remains."

"The poor creature looked most put out by the intrusion into its territory though, I thought," I added.

Barrett put his face in his hands. "This is terrible."

"It is also revenge," Holmes said quietly.

Barrett raised his head. "Revenge for what?"

"The pillaging of the tomb of Neb-Heka-Ra comes to mind. Not to mention the desecration of his corpse." Holmes paused and gave Barrett a hard look. "Not by any eldritch creature, but by human hands."

"It was an authorised excavation," Barrett said, fluffying up in indignation, like an irritated bantam cock whose territory has been invaded.

Holmes snorted. "Come, Mr. Barrett. We know about the ruse that got the government agent to leave the dig so that you could remove all of the tomb's contents, not just those items that you were permitted to take."

Barrett gaped at him. His mouth opened and closed, but no sound came out.

"Who assisted you, Mr. Barrett?" Lestrade asked. "That person may be in danger if they are here in London."

Barrett sighed. "It was Thierry Meylan, but…"

"He is already dead," Holmes said. "You told us yourself that he died in Italy."

Barrett nodded. "It was several days after we arrived in Naples. His daughter was distraught, or so I was told by one of Meylan's servants."

"His daughter?" I asked.

"Veronique. A pretty little thing, I believe. I never met her. I was told that she was very shy and of a retiring disposition. She went by the name of Veronique Meylan, but she wasn't entitled to it. She was the daughter of Thierry's Egyptian mistress. She was fortunate, in a way."

"How?" Lestrade asked.

"Thierry died in Italy," Barrett replied. "If he had died in Egypt, Veronique would have been left with nothing. As both a bastard and a woman, she could not have inherited. The Italians didn't care, so long as they got something in death taxes."

"Interesting," Holmes murmured. "You travelled to Naples with Meylan but did not meet his daughter?"

"She was already in Naples," Barrett replied. "Meylan sent her on ahead to open the house and get it ready for him. Several of their servants went with her, of course."

"How did Meylan die?" I asked.

"It was his stomach. The doctor in Naples said it was cholera."

"Did he?" Holmes said softly. "That is even more interesting." He looked sharply at Barrett. "What happened to Miss Meylan?"

Barrett shrugged. "Thierry had friends in Naples. I assume Veronique stayed with one of them whilst the funeral was being arranged. Probably stayed in Naples as well. There was nothing in Egypt for her to go back to, except a life on the streets. Her mother's family were unlikely to accept her."

I was beginning to develop quite a dislike for this irritating, selfish, young man.

"Did Joseph Brown have family?" Lestrade asked.

Barrett shrugged. "I have no idea. He never mentioned any."

"In that case, as his employer, you will need to arrange for the funeral." Lestrade said. "You will need to contact Dr. Bond at the Westminster Public Mortuary. Good day to you, sir." Lestrade turned on his heel and marched out of the room. Holmes and I followed.

When we reached to street. Holmes said softly to Lestrade. "You should not have let him get to you."

Lestrade snorted. "It was either walk out or punch him. The commissioner frowns on inspectors going around punching people."

"He is not a pleasant man," I observed.

"That level of self-absorption does not encourage the making of friends," Lestrade agreed. He looked at my friend. "What now, Holmes?"

"Now we visit Mr. Abasi Tarek. I feel our news will interest him greatly."

Abasi Tarek was in his office on the Strand when we arrived. Upon seeing us, he closed the office and ushered us upstairs to his rooms.

"It must be grave news indeed, Mr. Holmes," that brings you to my door.

"There has been another murder," my friend replied. "I also have a request of you."

"I shall endeavour to assist you to the best of my abilities. May I ask who has been murdered?" Tarek asked.

"Joseph Brown, Barrett's foreman of works and secretary. Did you know him?"

Tarek nodded. "Not personally, you understand. My master told me of him. It is believed that it was he who made the arrangements with Thierry Meylan." He paused. "How was Mr. Brown murdered?"

"The actual method is not known and is unlikely to be," Lestrade said. "The late Mr. Joseph Brown was found dismembered on the grounds of the manor of Lord Sebastian Clavering."

"Within the enclosure of His Lordship's pet crocodile, to be precise," Holmes said.

Tarek looked startled for a moment, and then nodded thoughtfully. "The curse, of course."

Holmes nodded.

Tarek looked at us all. "You do realize that this means there will be more murders?"

Lestrade nodded gloomily. "It stands to reason. The killers are following the pattern of the curse. Though for the life of me I cannot see how the last three will occur."

I frowned, "The last three?"

Holmes drew the sheet of paper on which Cavanagh had written out the curse from his pocket. "May the Blessed Lady Ma'at judge his soul; May Nehebkau cause his Ka and Ba to separate; and may Ammit devour his heart thus destroying him forever." He looked up. "I have to agree, Lestrade, that it will be difficult. Though no doubt our killers will find a way. They have been remarkably creative so far."

"Too blasted creative," I muttered.

"On the subject of killers, gentlemen," Tarek said. "My master has sent word that it is generally believed that Thierry Meylan was poisoned by his daughter."

"With arsenic," Holmes said.

Tarek stared at him. "How on earth did you know that, Mr. Holmes?"

"Barrett told us that it was his stomach and that the doctor in Naples said it was cholera. The symptoms of arsenical poisoning and cholera are remarkably similar."

"But not exactly the same," I added. "Those poisoned with arsenic often have reddened and swollen skin, which is not present in cholera. But if there is a cholera outbreak at the time, it is easy for a tired and overworked doctor to overlook that particular symptom."

Tarek nodded. "I understand that there is often cholera in Naples. As there once was in London."

"There are still outbreaks here occasionally," I said. "But not nearly as many as there were in the past."

This was thanks to Dr. John Snow who traced the source of a major cholera outbreak in Soho in 1854 to water from a pump in Broad Street. He curtailed the outbreak by removing the handle from the water pump. When the outbreak was stopped, the medical fraternity began to take seriously the idea that cholera was caused by contaminated water, not miasma or 'bad air' as they had been saying for centuries.

Abasi Tarek spoke again, drawing me out of my thoughts. "You said you had a request for me, Mr. Holmes?"

"I do. But first, do you know Veronique Meylan?"

"I have never met her formally, but I have seen her. Thierry Meylan was quite prominent in Cairo society and would take him daughter with him."

"Excellent. In that case I would be obliged if you would call again at our rooms in Baker Street tomorrow evening around 7 o'clock."

"Oh course, Mr. Holmes. If you think it will help."

"I think it will be most helpful, Mr. Tarek."

"Then I shall bid you gentlemen a good day and I shall see you tomorrow evening."

We took our leave of Abasi Tarek and went out onto the Strand.

As we got into the waiting growler, Lestrade asked "What was with all the questions regarding Miss Meylan?"

"Lestrade, Lestrade, Lestrade," Holmes chided gently. "Think, man."

Lestrade shook his head.

"And you a man of French Huguenot descent. The name of Veronique, when anglicized becomes Veronica."

I stared at my friend. "You think Lady Ashmoore is Veronique Meylan?"

"I think it is quite within the grounds of possibility," Holmes replied.

"But..."

"Think, Watson! Mycroft knows nothing about her except that Lord Ashmoore met her on the continent and married her."

"But even if what you suspect is true, how can she possibly be involved in the killings? Surely, she's not a..." I broke off.

"A murderess?" Holmes asked softly. "If the Khedive's information is correct, then she is guilty of at least one murder. That of her own father."

"What do we do now?" Lestrade asked in a strangely subdued voice.

"Now we get together the cast for a little play."

"And how do we do that?" I asked.

"We have a couple of places to visit," Holmes replied. "Lestrade, can you kindly ask the driver to take us to Jermyn Street."

Lestrade gave the order and then settled back into the seat.

"What is in Jermyn Street?" I asked.

"The office of Miss Cynthia Taverner," he replied.

"Who is this Miss Taverner," Lestrade asked.

"A female private enquiry agent whom Watson and I met briefly on another case," Holmes said. "She will be able to get where we cannot."

"And that is?" I asked.

"Close to Lady Veronica Ashmoore."

We sat in silence during the short ride to Jermyn Street.

We exited the growler outside a tailor's shop. Next to the shop was a door with a discreet plaque on it that read: Taverner's Private Enquiries: Discretion Guaranteed. Reasonable Rates. Apply Upstairs.

We filed upstairs and entered a tidy office with walls that were lined with heavy filing cabinets. A somewhat rickety desk sat in the middle of the room. A man with deep red hair, and aged somewhere between forty and fifty, looked up at us with pale blue eyes.

"Good afternoon, gentlemen, welcome to Taverner's Private Enquiries. How may we help you today?"

"Good afternoon," Holmes said. "May we speak with Miss Taverner?"

The man gave us a startled look, and then chuckled. "Ah, you know my employer then?"

"Dr. Watson and I have worked with Miss Taverner before."

The man rose from his desk and held out his hand. "Mr.

Sherlock Holmes, I presume. A pleasure to meet you sir. I am Robert Boscombe. Miss Taverner's clerk." He looked enquiringly at Lestrade and me.

Holmes gestured to each of this. "This is Dr. Watson, and this is Inspector Lestrade."

Mr. Boscombe shook both our hands. "A real pleasure, gentlemen. I read your cases in the *Strand Magazine*, Doctor. Extremely interesting. Inspector Lestrade, I follow your cases in the *Police Gazette* with great interest. It is an honour to make the acquaintance of you both."

We murmured our thanks with no little modicum of embarrassment.

"Is Miss Taverner in?" Holmes asked.

Mr. Boscombe shook his head. "I am afraid not. She is out with a client. May I take a message?"

Holmes nodded. "Will you ask Miss Taverner to come to 221B Baker Street tomorrow evening at 7 o'clock? We have need of her assistance." He paused. "At her usual rates, of course."

Boscombe sat back down at his desk and carefully made a note of the time and place. He looked up at Holmes. "I shall inform Miss Taverner as soon as she returns to the office."

"Thank you, Mr. Boscombe. Much obliged."

We left the office and went back downstairs to where the growler waited.

"Anywhere else, Holmes?" Lestrade asked. "Otherwise, I shall drop you both back at Baker Street before heading back to the Yard."

Holmes frowned. "One more visit, I think."

"To where?" I asked.

"The Diogenes Club."

"To appraise your brother of the latest murder?" Lestrade asked.

"I am sure Mycroft has already heard about that, Lestrade," Holmes replied. "No, I wish to ask him for his help."

"His help?" I asked.

"Well, not his help per se, but rather the help of one of his people."

"Who?" I asked curiously.

"I think this case needs an extra feminine touch, Watson."

Lestrade grinned widely. "You want to ask him to lend us Dorothy?"

Holmes nodded. "I feel Miss Watts could be very useful in this case.

I must admit I was rather pleased at Holmes's idea. I was rather fond of Dorothy Watts. Dorothy, born Daniel, had been of great assistance in the case I have referred to previously as *The Molly-Boy Murders*, and had saved my life in somewhat dramatic circumstances. It was the same case that had involved

Lord Francis Harkness's cousin, Sir Lucas Catterick. At the end of the case, Mycroft Holmes had taken Dorothy into his employ as one of his agents.

Mycroft was obviously expecting us, as tea was waiting for us in the Stranger's Room. Over an excellent cup of Darjeeling tea and several roast beef sandwiches, Holmes filled his brother in on the events of the day.

Though, as Holmes had observed earlier, Mycroft was already aware of the gruesome discovery at Lord Sebastian Clavering's Richmond manor.

"A bad business, this, Sherlock," Mycroft observed, taking a sip from his cup. "Am I to take it that you wish for my assistance with this case?"

"Not yours, brother," Holmes said.

Mycroft smiled briefly. "Dorothy."

"Exactly," Holmes replied. "It is looking more and more as if Lady Veronica Ashmoore may be heavily involved in this case. We cannot get close to her..."

"But Dorothy can," Mycroft said.

"Along with Miss Taverner," Holmes said.

"The private enquiry agent," I added.

Mycroft nodded thoughtfully. "When do you need Dorothy's services?"

"If you can spare her, please get her to come to Baker Street at 7 o'clock tomorrow night. There is a meeting for all involved."

"Dorothy will be there," Mycroft said.

We thanked him and took our leave. Lestrade had the growler take us back to Baker Street.

Mrs. Hudson met us as we came through the door, an envelope clutched in her hand.

"Mr. Holmes, this came for you about an hour ago."

"Thank you, Mrs. Hudson," Holmes said as he took the envelope from her hand.

"I'll bring dinner up directly."

Holmes and I went up to our rooms, and Holmes placed the envelope on his desk unopened.

I nodded towards it. "Are you not going to open it?"

"After dinner," my friend replied. "It is from Lord Sebastian Clavering."

"How do you know that?"

"The seal on the back of the envelope is an S entwined with a C. The initials of Lord Clavering. Not to mention the Clavering coat of arms in the top left corner."

"Then it is likely to be important," I said.

Holmes shook his head. "It is most likely the names that I asked for."

"Names?"

"Of those who knew that Lord Clavering had a Nile crocodile."

Further discussion was interrupted by Mrs. Hudson bringing in dinner, which was roast mutton with stewed mushrooms in brown gravy, spinach dressed with cream and flavoured with salt, sugar, and nutmeg, and turnips mashed with butter, cream, and salt. This was accompanied by Mrs. Hudson's fine homemade bread with sweet butter. We were eating our pudding of plum tart with wine sauce when Holmes deigned to open the letter from Lord Clavering.

He scanned it for a moment. "It is as I suspected, Watson, Lord Clavering has supplied me with a list of those who knew of the existence of Sobek."

"Which must surely shrink the list of suspects," I commented.

Holmes nodded. "It does indeed. Lord Clavering says that Lord Francis Harkness, Mr. Albert Granger, and Lord Reginald Ashmoore all knew about the crocodile."

"What about Lady Veronica Ashmoore?" I asked.

Holmes looked back at me. "If you remember Lord Clavering said that Lord Ashmoore brought his wife with him to Clavering House to view the beast."

I sat back in my chair. "I had forgotten that he said that. So, she knew."

"She did."

I sighed.

Holmes looked at me with some sympathy. "I know that you are reluctant to think ill of the fair sex, my friend. Indeed, your own goodness does you credit. But never think for one moment that the female of the species is any less deadly than the male. In nature, the female is often more so than the male."

"I know, Holmes. It is just that the nature of these crimes..." my voice tailed off.

Holmes nodded thoughtfully. "They are gruesome, even for a man. The thought that a woman could be responsible for them strikes you to the heart."

I shook my head. "You know me too well, Holmes."

Holmes shook himself. "Come, Watson, enough of these gloomy thoughts. You are starting to take a leaf out of my book."

I laughed at the very idea that I could become like Holmes. There was only one Sherlock Holmes. I got to my feet to pour us both a brandy, and we spent the rest of the evening in a companionable manner.

Chapter Twelve

The next day was spent quietly. Holmes cajoled Mrs. Hudson into baking for our guests that evening, then went back to studying his own notes and papers, and the pieces of rope he had acquired.

Perceiving that I was surplus to requirements, I informed Mrs. Hudson that I would be back before our guests arrived and took myself to my club for a few games of billiards, and a meal. I walked back to Baker Street, arriving home around 6.30 p.m.

I walked into our rooms to find Holmes rearranging the furniture. He took in my expression with a slight smile. "We cannot expect people to sit upon the floor, Watson."

I looked around the room. Our four dining chairs had been arranged around the room joining our small couch and two armchairs. "Seating for eight people, Holmes? Surely there will only be six of us."

Holmes shook his head. "Mr. Boscombe will come with Miss Taverner. He will most likely use the excuse that a young lady should not travel in cabs unescorted in the evenings."

"That still leaves one extra chair," I observed.

"Mycroft," Holmes replied.

I gave my friend a startled look. "Your brother is a creature of habit. What makes you think he will come here tonight?"

"Curiosity, my friend."

"Curiosity killed the cat, according to the old proverb," I said dryly.

Holmes flashed a look of amusement at me. "Curiosity will also bring Mycroft out of the Diogenes Club for the evening. Curiosity is about the only thing that Mycroft has in common with a feline."

Just before 7 o'clock I heard a cab draw up downstairs. Looking out of the window I saw Lestrade alight, pay the cabby, and come into the building.

He had not even entered our rooms before I heard the sound of other vehicles arriving.

Right behind Lestrade came Miss Cynthia Taverner, accompanied by her clerk Robert Boscombe.

"I do hope you do not mind me accompanying Miss Taverner," Boscombe said. "I felt that I could not, in all good conscience allow my employer to travel alone at night in a cab. Dreadful things happen to women alone at night."

"Not at all, Mr. Boscombe," I said.

Holmes gave me a faint smile.

I had met Miss Taverner briefly during a case involving jewel thefts and a politician. Cynthia Taverner was a pretty, young, woman with dark hair, brown eyes that sparkled with merriment, and a charming dimple. She was the cousin of Frederick Taverner, M.P., a somewhat roguish chap whose antics belied his sharp intellect. An intellect that his cousin shared.

Holmes showed Miss Taverner to the small couch and Mr. Boscombe to a chair beside it. Lestrade had already seated himself in one of the other dining chairs.

The next person to arrive was Abasi Tarek. Holmes swiftly introduced him to the others, and he seated himself on one of the dining chairs next to Lestrade.

The sound of another carriage, followed by a distinctly heavy tread on the stairs, told me that, once again, Holmes was correct. His brother Mycroft had chosen to accompany Dorothy to the meeting.

Mycroft took one of the armchairs and Dorothy was seated beside Miss Taverner.

Looking at them sitting side by side, they could almost have been sisters. Dorothy was quite petite with curly brown hair, and doe-like brown eyes. The two women gave each other a measuring look, before nodding and turning their attention back to the room.

Holmes cleared his throat, drawing everyone's attention to him. He looked at Miss Taverner and Dorothy. "Do I need to explain the case, ladies?"

Dorothy shook her head. "Not to me. Your brother gave me the details on the way. I believe you need some small assistance with the murder of Dr. Simpson and subsequent murders?"

"Nor to me," added Miss Taverner. "I have been following the story in the papers. And yes, Mr. Holmes, I do know that the papers sensationalize things. I do, however, have my own contacts in Scotland Yard."

"And how is Inspector Gregson these days?" Holmes asked.

"As annoying as ever," Miss Taverner replied. "But still a useful source of information."

Holmes gave a dry little chuckle. "Well then, I shall explain our little problem. We have a possible suspect for the killings. And that suspect is Lady Veronica Ashmoore."

"Lady Ashmoore?" Boscombe looked startled. "A titled lady a vicious killer?"

"Not by herself, Mr. Boscombe," Holmes replied. "But most certainly the guiding force behind the killings."

Cynthia Taverner looked thoughtful. "You need someone to get close to the lady."

"Indeed," Holmes said. "Whilst I have masqueraded as a woman on many occasions, I cannot convincingly carry off the class of woman that would be able to get close to Lady Veronica. Nor am I the right age to encourage confidences from a young wife."

Both Cynthia and Dorothy nodded at this. Dorothy looked thoughtful. "The most usual reason for woman to call upon one another is raising funds for a particular charity. What charity could get us close to Lady Veronica?"

"The lady in question is foreign," Lestrade said. "I doubt she will be much interested in any charity here."

"What about the East End Mission for the Children of Poor Immigrant Workers?" Dorothy asked. "I have come across numerous people from that charity several times in my work."

Mycroft nodded. "One of the founders is a member of the Diogenes Club. I shall smooth the way for you. In case Lady Veronica gets suspicious and makes inquiries."

"I can borrow a carriage from Freddie," Cynthia said. "He will be happy to lend us a coachman as well. And perhaps a footman in case of trouble?"

Holmes shook his head. "Yes to the coach, but not the footman. I should like Mr. Tarek to fill that role."

Abasi Tarek looked startled. "Me? Whatever for?"

"It would hopefully give you an opportunity to get a look at Lady Veronica."

"But why would I...?" Tarek stopped and looked thoughtful for a moment. "You think that Lady Veronica Ashmoore is someone else. Someone I may recognize."

"I do," Holmes replied gravely.

"You think this Lady Ashmoore is Veronique Meylan."

"I do," Holmes said again.

"I shall be delighted to assist," Tarek replied.

Dorothy tapped her right index finger against her chin, deep in thought. "Do we go as women of equal rank? Or should I be Miss Taverner's companion?"

"We go as friends," Miss Taverner said firmly.

Dorothy gave her a strange look. "Thank you. Miss Taverner."

"Call me Cynthia, Miss Watts," Miss Taverner replied with a smile. "We are friends, after all."

Dorothy gave her a smile of her own. "I do believe you are correct. Thank you, Cynthia."

"You are most welcome, Dorothy."

"This is going to take some time to arrange," Lestrade observed. "At least two days, by the time the carriage is available, and a time to call on Lady Ashmoore is arranged."

Cynthia nodded. "Leave it with us, Inspector Lestrade." She looked at Dorothy and at Abasi Tarek. "The three of us shall come to Baker Street as soon as we have something for you. I do not anticipate it taking longer than two days. Three at the most."

With a plan settled on, everyone but Lestrade took their leave. Lestrade accepted the glass of whisky that I handed him with a nod of thanks. He took a sip. "Do you think they will be successful?"

"I am sure of it," Holmes replied. "Miss Taverner and Miss Watts are exceptionally talented."

"The real question is, I suppose, will they be successful before there is another murder," Lestrade said gloomily.

"That, my dear Lestrade, is not a question that I am in a position to answer," Holmes replied softly.

Chapter Thirteen

That particular question was answered rather abruptly the next morning when a police constable arrived on our doorstep with a message from Lestrade requesting our presence in Kensington.

It was starting to rain slightly, so Holmes took his sturdy umbrella from the hall stand as we left.

As we approached in the growler, I recognized the house. It was the home of the banker, Mr. Robert Wilson, of Wilson & Son Commercial Bank. The man who had provided much of the funding for the expedition.

Lestrade was standing on the front steps of the house, his face as white as a freshly laundered sheet. I exchanged a concerned look with Holmes as we exited the growler.

"Is it worse than Brown's death, Lestrade?" Holmes asked softly.

Lestrade shook his head. "Not as such. It's just..." He paused. "You had best see for yourselves."

We were led into the house. Somewhere in the distance I could hear a woman wailing. I assumed that it was Mrs. Wilson. I could not help but wince at the sound.

"I have sent a constable for the local doctor," Lestrade said softly. "The lady is in genuine distress. Especially as she found the body."

Lestrade led us to a small study close by the room where we had spoken with the Wilsons not too many days ago.

Robert Wilson lay in a heap upon the floor. I could tell at a glance that his death had not been an easy one. His face was twisted in a rictus of pain. A strange sandy coloured rope lay at his feet.

Holmes immediately went into a defensive stance, his still furled umbrella extended.

"It is dead," Lestrade said, shuddering slightly. "I hate snakes!"

"Did you kill it?" Holmes asked.

Lestrade shook his head. "No. It was dead when we arrived.

I came close enough to realize that what I had taken to be an odd sort of rope, was the corpse of a large snake, perhaps some five or six feet in length.

"What on earth is it?" I asked.

"I am no herpetologist," Holmes said. "But I very much suspect that that is a specimen of *Naja Haje,* otherwise known as the Egyptian cobra. Highly venomous, bringing death due to respiratory failure in a very short time."

"That bloody curse," Lestrade swore.

"Indeed," Holmes replied.

"May the Cobra of Uajyt strike his heel," I murmured. "Was Mr. Wilson bitten on the heel?"

Holmes stepped forward, using his umbrella to lift the legs of Wilson's trousers. He leaned forward. "That is not a snake bite," he observed.

I joined him, carefully avoiding the snake corpse. While I did not have a horror of them, as Lestrade appeared to have, the time I had spent in India, not to mention the dreadful case of *The Speckled Band* that Holmes and I had dealt with some years before, where Dr. Grimesby Roylott had murdered one of his stepdaughters with a snake and had attempted to do the same with the other, only to fall victim to his own vicious pet serpent, had left me with a certain wariness around the creatures.

I bent over the dead man, frowning slightly. "The man has only one puncture mark. He was not bitten by the cobra, but instead injected with its venom."

"How is that possible?" Lestrade asked.

"Snake venom has its uses, Lestrade," Holmes replied. "In ancient times, for example, arrow heads were dipped in snake venom, making even a scratch from an arrow a fatal wound. I suspect when we examine that cobra closely, we will find that the venom sacs have been removed."

Lestrade frowned. "So, our killers killed the snake, removed the venom sacs…"

"Put the venom into a syringe," I added.

"Then came here, overpowered Mr. Wilson," Lestrade continued.

Holmes again raised the trouser cuff. "You will note that Mr. Wilson was also tied up like the others." He pointed to red rope marks around the victim's ankles.

"Then they injected him with the venom, waited for him to die, and left the corpse of the snake behind to drive the message home."

"Exactly, Lestrade," Holmes gave the inspector a look of approval. He looked back down at the body. "They have also made a major mistake."

"And that is?" Lestrade asked.

"They left us the means to find them and the evidence to convict them."

"What?" I exclaimed. "But how?"

Holmes leaned forward and carefully picked up the dead snake. "This poor creature. There are not too many places in London where one can acquire exotic animals. In fact, I can only think of one who would be able to supply an Egyptian cobra."

There was the sound of someone at the outside door, a murmur of voices, followed by footsteps. A uniformed police constable poked his head around the door. "Excuse me, sir, but the local doctor has arrived. I have sent him upstairs to attend to Mrs. Wilson."

"Thank you, Jamieson," Lestrade replied. "And tell the housekeeper that we want to talk to anyone who may have heard something last night. As for Mrs. Wilson." Lestrade paused. "We will leave talking to her until her doctor tells us she is up to it. I do not want to push the lady further into hysterics."

The constable nodded and withdrew. We waited in

silence for the arrival of Dr. Bond and his assistants. Holmes prowled the room. I stood beside the corpse of the late Mr. Robert Wilson. Lestrade stood as far away from the snake as he was able to and still remain in the same room.

Dr. Bond arrived perhaps thirty minutes later. He nodded to us in greeting and stooped to examine the body. The man looked up at Lestrade. "You do bring me the most interesting corpses, Inspector. It makes a change from suicides and the victims of drunken brawls." He looked back down at the body, a little sadly, I thought. "Mind you, it is not necessarily a good change."

The doctor looked at the snake, eyebrows raised. "Do you want me to take that with us?"

"If you could, please, Dr. Bond," Holmes said. "We would be grateful if you could get someone to examine it closely."

Dr. Bond frowned, then his brow cleared. "I have a contact in the natural history department of the British Museum. I shall get him to send someone down to the morgue to examine the snake. Do I ask him what to look for?"

"Ask him to check if the venom sacs are still in place and send word either to me at Baker Street or Lestrade at Scotland Yard."

Dr. Bond nodded and sent one of his assistants to fetch a sack to put the snake in.

Constable Jamieson reappeared. "Excuse me, sir, but

the housekeeper is here. Do you want to have a word with her?"

"Of course. We will come out."

"There is no need, Inspector." A robust matronly woman firmly inserted herself into the room."

"Madam," Lestrade exclaimed. Looking quickly to where Dr. Bond and his assistants were gathered around her employer's corpse. "You should not be in here!"

"I have been in service for many years, Inspector. I have seen more than one dead body in my time."

"I should imagine you have," Holmes said with a slight smile, coming forward. "I am Mr. Sherlock Holmes," he gestured towards me. "And this is Dr. John Watson. May I ask your name?"

"I am Mrs. Diana Myers. Housekeeper and cook to the Wilsons. And before you ask, there is no Mr. Myers, it is a courtesy title only."

I nodded. It was common practice for women in senior household positions such as housekeeper or cook to be given the honorific, even though very few of them were married. Married woman, except long-term retainers on country estates, tended to leave service upon marriage. Employers seemed to prefer it that way, and to be honest, many men did not care for their wives to be working outside of the marital home.

Lestrade recovered himself and joined the conversation. "Did you hear anything last night, ma'am?"

"No, Inspector. I was not in a position to do so. I am

135

housekeeper and cook for the household and my rooms are right to the back of the house. Unless the bell is rung for service, I would not hear anything. And at night, the bell would not be rung. Mr. Wilson was quite firm on that. If business guests were expected late, food would be put out and Mr. Wilson would serve them himself."

"Were guests expected last night?" Lestrade asked.

Mrs. Myers shook her head. "No, Inspector. It was something quite rare. Mr. Wilson preferred to do his business at the bank. Though he did make exceptions for special clients."

"For ones such as Lord Ashmoore, perhaps?" Lestrade asked.

"I do not know the names of any of Mr. Wilson's clients."

"Would anyone else have heard anything?" Holmes asked.

Mrs. Myers shook her head again. "No, Mr. Holmes. The Wilson's have very few live-in staff. I live in because I am both housekeeper and cook. But there is no butler, and no footmen. The coachman and the stable lads all live in the mews out the back, and the maids are all day-girls. They come in at 6 a.m. and leave around 6 p.m. All local so they can get home without danger. It is not safe in this city for young girls to be wandering around alone after dark."

"So, no witnesses," Lestrade said with a sigh

"I am afraid not, Inspector."

"Thank you for your time, Mrs. Myers."

The lady bobbed a slight curtsey and left the room.

Lestrade looked at Holmes. "Well, now what do we do?"

"We follow the clues, Lestrade," my friend replied.

"And where exactly are the clues leading us?" Lestrade asked.

"To Jamrach's Animal Emporium," Holmes said.

Chapter Fourteen

Jamrach's Animal Emporium had several locations around London. There was a warehouse on Old Gravel Lane in Southwark, a menagerie in Betts Street in Tower Hamlets, and the main business premises on Ratcliffe Highway in Wapping. All of the sites were perfectly situated to house animals straight off the docks with minimal stress to the creatures.

The firm had been started by Charles Jamrach's father, Johann Gottlieb Jamrach, in Antwerp and he had extended the business to London. His eldest son Anton had taken over the London end of the firm, but he died young leaving his younger brother Charles to build the business into an awe-inspiring success. Jamrach's Animal Emporium supplied the zoological gardens at Regent's Park, as well as selling to noblemen such as Lord Clavering, and supplying travelling circuses. The artist and poet Dante Gabriel Rossetti had purchased his pet wombat, Top, from Jamrach's.

If most people knew of Jamrach's Animal Emporium, it was because of an event in 1857 when a Bengal Tiger escaped from its box at the Ratcliffe Highway premises. A small child approached and tried to pet the animal, never having seen such a large cat before. The tiger, unfortunately, thought the boy was lunch, and snatched him up. Charles Jamrach raced up and thrust his bare hands down the tiger's throat, forcing the animal to release its prey.

It was to the Ratcliffe Highway premises that we headed. Being the main business address, it was where we were most likely to obtain answers to our questions.

The premises were fine and clean, but a heavy animal smell hung over the area. An amplified scent of animal dung, raw meat, damp straw, and wet fur, caused a miasma that was not particularly pleasant. Various animal noises could be faintly heard. I thought I heard the roar of a lion and knowing that Lord Clavering had purchased his tiger here, I decided that I probably was not mistaken.

I realized that the mixture of noise and noisome smell was another reason the main business was hard by the Thames. With all the warehouses down here, there were few neighbours to be discommoded by the less than salubrious scents.

A pretty green parrot with a flash of yellow feathers at its neck eyed us from its perch in a large cage as we entered the building, before letting out a stream of profanity that would have made a sailor blush.

A bright-eyed young man came hurrying out of a back room. He snatched up a blanket which he threw over the cage, before whisking it away to where he came from.

He returned to us a moment later. "Welcome to Jamrach's Animal Emporium, gentlemen. I apologise for Solomon. He's a yellow-naped Amazon parrot that we purchased off a sailor who bought him in Guatemala. Unfortunately, we didn't discover his appalling vocabulary until after we purchased him. I do not think we will be able to sell him. He should never have been out the front, but parrots get destructive if they're bored, so we sit him out here for a few hours each day." The man paused and wiped his face with his handkerchief. "How may I help you today?"

Lestrade stepped forward. "I am Inspector Lestrade of Scotland Yard. These gentlemen are Mr. Sherlock Holmes and Doctor John Watson." He gestured to each of us in turn. "We have a few questions about an animal purchase."

The young man gave Lestrade an incredulous look. "Can you prove you are whom you say you are?"

Lestrade raised an eyebrow. "I have not had to do this for a while," he commented. He reached into his coat and withdrew his warrant card. The police issued each officer a card when they joined, with the cards being reissued when the holder was promoted. The initial warrant card number, however, remained the same.

The young man studied the card carefully, before handing it back to Lestrade. "My apologies, Inspector Lestrade. We take the privacy of our clients very seriously. The number of reporters who come here trying to find out who has purchased what is ridiculous."

"A commendable stance to take," Holmes commented.

"Thank you, sir."

"Do you need us to prove whom we are?" I asked.

The young man shook his head. "That will not be necessary, sir. The inspector has proved who he is. That is sufficient. You are obviously all here in an official capacity." He looked back at Lestrade. "Please ask your questions, inspector."

"We might start with your name," Lestrade said dryly.

"I apologise. I have been remiss. I am Henry Prince."

"Well, Mr. Prince, we have a query regarding the purchaser of an Egyptian cobra."

"An Egyptian cobra?"

"Yes," said Holmes. "A fine specimen of N*aja Haje*, around six feet in length. It would have been purchased relatively recently. If you could check your records for us..."

"I have no need to do that, Mr. Holmes," Mr. Prince interjected. "We have only sold one example of that particular serpent in recent months."

"You remember who it was sold to?" Lestrade asked.

Prince nodded. "Yes, Inspector. Mostly because it is unusual to sell venomous snakes to members of the aristocracy. They tend to prefer things like lions or cheetahs."

"Or crocodiles?" I asked.

Henry Prince smiled briefly. "You are familiar with Lord Sebastian Clavering, I take it? His Lordship is a bit of an outlier, I must admit. He tends to prefer the unusual."

"Like Sobek and Priscilla," Holmes said.

Prince outright laughed. "It does make finding creatures for him interesting," the man admitted. "But as to the cobra, as I said, we have only sold one recently. To Lady Veronica Ashmoore."

"You were right, Holmes," Lestrade murmured.

"Did Her Ladyship collect the cobra herself?" Holmes

141

asked.

Henry Prince shook his head. "No, she sent two manservants to collect it. Two Egyptian men. Masuda and Waaiz were their names."

"Was that Lady Ashmoore's only purchase?" I asked.

Prince shook his head. "No, Doctor. She has another on order."

"And that is?" Lestrade asked eagerly.

"Lady Ashmoore has asked us to obtain a prime example of *Neophron Percnopterus*, otherwise known as the Egyptian vulture."

"Will her servants be collecting it?" Holmes asked.

"Not this time. Lady Ashmoore has left instructions to be informed when it arrives and has left an address for it to be delivered to."

"We shall need two things from you," Holmes said. "The delivery address, and for you to send word to us when the bird arrives and when it is being delivered."

"Of course, sir."

Holmes handed over one of his cards to Mr. Prince and we left the building.

"What now, Holmes?" I asked.

"Now, my dear Watson, we pay a little visit to the Ashmoores."

"To interview the manservants?" Lestrade asked.

Holmes frowned. "I think not. To do so would most likely alert Lady Ashmoore to the fact we know about her. I would rather keep Her Ladyship in ignorance for the moment."

Lestrade nodded. "That makes sense. At the moment all we know for a certainty is that Lady Ashmoore purchased the cobra. We have no evidence that she used its venom to kill Robert Wilson."

"Exactly, Lestrade."

We got back into the growler and headed out to the Ashmoores' elegant house in Chiswick.

The butler let us in and led us to the library where we had met Lord Reginald Ashmoore on our previous visit. He disappeared for a few minutes before coming back to escort us to the man himself.

Lord Ashmoore was outside at the rear of the house, overseeing the packing of a carriage. He gave us an extremely grumpy look as we approached.

"We do apologise for not making an appointment," Holmes said smoothly, harking back to His Lordship's sarcastic comment on our previous visit, "...but murder so rarely makes an appointment."

"What do you want?" he snapped.

"To let you know that you will be in need of another

banker for any further expeditions," Lestrade said.

"What do you mean?"

"Robert Wilson has been murdered," I said.

Lord Ashmoore's jaw dropped. "What?"

"He was injected with cobra venom," Lestrade said.

"The venom of an Egyptian cobra, to be precise," Holmes added.

Lord Ashmoore slumped, like a puppet with cut strings. "Maybe my wife is correct."

"About what?" Holmes asked softly.

"That there really is a curse."

"There are no supernatural forces at work here, Lord Ashmoore," Holmes said. "Only very human agencies with extremely nasty, not to say inventive, minds. Robert Wilson was not bitten by a cobra. Someone went to a great deal of effort to obtain a cobra, kill it, remove its venom sacs, and inject Wilson with the contents."

"But still…" Lord Ashmoore trailed off and looked at the carriage. "My wife is afraid. She wants us to go into hiding. I will not. But I am letting my wife go."

"Go where?" Holmes said sharply.

"If I tell you…" he started to object.

"If you tell us," Holmes said smoothly, "then Lestrade here can organize discreet protection. Some lads who can watch over your good lady without her being aware."

Lestrade opened his mouth to object, but I hurriedly stood on his foot. I realized that Holmes must have a plan in mind, and he did not need our friend blundering in. Lestrade shot me a filthy look but closed his mouth.

Lord Ashmoore suddenly smiled. I realized then that the man truly loved his wife. He was in for a harsh awaking and a load of heartbreak when the truth was revealed.

The address His Lordship gave us was for a house in Islington. Quite a way from Chiswick, but much closer to the beating heart of London. "It was my *pied-à-terre* in my youth," Lord Ashmoore explained. "A quiet place away from my father and his more boisterous activities." He indicated two men that came out of the house carrying luggage. "Masuda and Waaiz will look after my wife. They have been servants of her family since they were children. Masuda's wife, Dina, is also going with them. She will cook for them and act as lady's maid to my wife. I offered to send more servants, but as my dear wife pointed out, there really is not the room for them."

I saw Holmes look intently at the men, and then at Lady Veronica who followed them out. The lady looked stunning in a fashionable tea gown in a deep shade of blue. She greeted us politely as she came to stand beside her husband. A less fashionably dressed woman came out of the house and was helped into the carriage by one of the men. I suspected that this was Dina. One of the men climbed onto the back of the coach, and the other seated himself on the driver's seat. Without another word they departed. Lord and Lady Ashmoore watched the carriage leave.

I was a little puzzled that Lady Ashmoore had not gone with them and said so. She smiled at my puzzlement. "My servants will get the house set up for me and return for me tomorrow."

"Besides which, my love, you do have an appointment tomorrow morning," Lord Ashmoore said. He turned to us. "Some ladies from the East End Mission for the Children of Poor Immigrant Workers have asked to meet with my wife, no doubt to garner her aid for some project." His expression clouded, "Unless you think it is not a good idea? Having strangers come to the house?"

Holmes shook his head. "I have heard of that mission. They do good work amongst the poor. I am sure that you will have nothing to fear from a visit."

Lord Ashmoore nodded. "You are correct of course. I am worrying over much. After all, a woman could not be responsible these foul murders."

There was nothing we could say to that, so we took our leave of the house. Out on the street, Lestrade turned to Holmes, his moustache twitching in indignation. "Men to watch the house? How in Heaven's name do you expect me to get permission for that? We do not have enough evidence to arrest Lady Ashmoore! The commissioner is not going to want to get involved until it is crystal clear that she is the killer. Even if she is the only possible person."

Holmes chuckled dryly at Lestrade's mild theatrics.

"Calm yourself, my good Lestrade. I said, '*some* lads,' I did not specify that they would be police."

"You mean…?"

"It sounds like a perfect job for the Baker Street Irregulars, does it not, Watson?"

"It does indeed, Holmes," I said with a small smile.

"Now," Holmes said. "Time to pay Mr. Bernard Barrett a visit, then back to Baker Street. I shall contemplate the ears later."

I blinked. "Ears, Holmes?"

"Ears, my dear Watson, they will be crucial to this case."

Lestrade glared at him. "You are chaffing me!"

"I assure you, Lestrade, that I am quite serious. Come, we must be off."

Lestrade looked at me. I shrugged my incomprehension and followed Holmes to the growler. Still muttering to himself, Lestrade followed me. He sat glaring at Holmes all the way back to Marylebone and the rooms of Bernard Barrett.

Bernard Barrett was not pleased to see us. He glared at us as we entered the room. "It is all your fault," he shouted.

Holmes raised an eyebrow in query. "What is?"

"That I cannot raise the funds for another expedition to Egypt. Nor can I get any response from the Egyptian government to my requests for permits."

"You rather did that to yourself, Mr. Barrett," Lestrade said. "When you ignored the restrictions placed on you in favour of robbing the tomb of Neb-Heka-Ra for Lord Ashmoore."

"Rubbish!" Barrett snarled. "That blaggard that calls himself the Khedive has no right to tell me, an Englishman, what I can and cannot do. No right to keep me out of Egypt. He is only there on the sufferance of our government any way."

Holmes looked at the man in disgust. "We came here to warn you…"

"Get out! I want no warnings from you!"

Holmes looked at him for a long moment, and then dipped his head in acknowledgement. "Very well. On your own head be it." He turned on his heel and walked out the door. Lestrade and I followed.

Back in the growler, we sat in silence for the brief ride back to Baker Street. As we got out of the carriage, Holmes turned to Lestrade. "Do come in, Lestrade. We need to discuss what is happening, and we may as well do it in comfort over a pot of tea and some of Mrs. Hudson's excellent baked goods."

One of the Irregulars was, as per usual, lurking close by. As we went to enter the building, Holmes nodded to him, indicating that assistance was needed. The boy grinned and raced off, no doubt to get hold of Wiggins, the acknowledged leader of the Baker Street Irregulars.

"Mrs. Hudson," Holmes called as we entered.

Our landlady came out of her suite of rooms. "Yes, Mr. Holmes?" She smiled at our friend. "Hello, Inspector Lestrade."

The inspector removed his hat. "A pleasure to see you again, ma'am."

Lestrade, living a bachelor existence in rented rooms in a lodging house close by Scotland Yard, was much admired by our landlady. Mostly for his appreciation of her cooking. This had resulted in a mild flirtation between them at times, which amused Holmes and me.

"Mrs. Hudson," Holmes said, "we have need of tea and whatever light comestibles you may have at hand." He gave her an arch look. "Wiggins will be joining us as well."

Mrs. Hudson shook her head. She was much more accepting of the Irregulars now that it was only Wiggins who came to the house. In the early days the hordes of grubby urchins had raised her ire, resulting in her raising her voice to Holmes. "I am sure I can arrange ample refreshments."

We headed upstairs to our rooms, removing coats and hats, and making ourselves comfortable.

As we seated ourselves, Holmes said, "We have much to discuss, but I would rather wait until the Irregulars have been set to work."

Lestrade shrugged. "As long as I can go back to the Yard with some form of a plan for the superintendent, I don't mind how long we wait."

A knocking at the door downstairs heralded the arrival of Wiggins. A lean lad of indeterminate age, he fairly bounced into the room, his eyes bright with anticipation.

Mrs. Hudson followed him in bearing a heavily laden tea tray, which I hastened to relieve her of.

The tray certainly contained ample refreshments. Alongside slices of Victoria sponge, there were plates of carraway seed biscuits, lavender biscuits, and ginger biscuits. Mrs. Hudson then returned with another tray containing scones with bowls of jam and cream, and a large plate of egg and water cress, and beef and pickle, sandwiches. Lestrade took that tray from her and placed it on the table beside the first.

Holmes poured tea for us all and made sure that Wiggins had a plate that mostly contained sandwiches, though I notice that he added a large scone with a generous helping of jam and cream to the selection. Wiggins beamed at us, clearly delighted with this bounty.

Holmes took a sip of his tea and said to the attentive Wiggins. "I have a job for the Irregulars. I need lads to watch two addresses and let me know immediately when any movement occurs. It will need to be round the clock observation. Have you enough lads for that, Wiggins?"

Wiggins took a large bite from his beef and pickle sandwich and chewed thoughtfully for a moment. Then he nodded. "Got several new lads. We only takes the best, Mr. 'Olmes, yer knows that. Yer reckon we runs two atta time, changin' every couple o' 'ours would do it?"

"How many Irregulars do you have at the moment?" Lestrade asked.

"There's me, an' Timmy, an' Jackie, an' Rob, an' Scruffy Bob, an' Tom, an' Jonesie, an' Fred, an' Liz, an' Molly, an' Jenny, an' Mick."

"That is twelve," Holmes said. "You should be able to manage it."

"Liz, Molly, and Jenny?" I asked. "You have girls running with you now, Wiggins?"

"Yep, Doc. Working for Mr. 'Olmes we sometimes needs t' get t' places where a bloke can't rightly get."

"Are you sure they won't get hurt?" I asked.

Wiggins laughed. "Ain't no cove stupid enough t' try. Molly once punched a rozzer in the tallywags, an' Jenny bit a bloke's hand clear t' the bone when 'e tried to grab 'er. An' Liz ain't no girl. Liz is short for lizard. 'E can get in t' all sorts of places like a lizard can. 'Is real name is Joe, but 'e don't answer t' that." He turned to Holmes. "Will that be all, Mr. 'Olmes?"

"Yes, it is, Wiggins."

Wiggins and one or two of the other Irregulars could read, so Holmes carefully wrote out the addresses of Barrett's flat and Ashmoore's Islington house for the lad. Though the law stated all children should get an education, the reality of

151

poverty in London meant that very few working class, and lower working class, children ever learned more than how to write their name and to add a few numbers. When it came to the children of the streets, like the Irregulars, the number of them that were even marginally literate dropped even further. Wiggins would see to it that everyone knew exactly where the addresses were.

Wiggins nodded to us and stood up to leave. He gave the plate of biscuits a wistful look.

Holmes got to his feet as well. Digging into his pocket he pulled out some coins which he gave to Wiggins. He then took a napkin from the table and wrapped up the biscuits which he gave to Wiggins with a conspiratorial wink.

Wiggins grinned at him. "Thankee kindly, Mr. 'Olmes." He carefully placed the napkin full of treats inside his coat pocket then sauntered out of the door.

"What Mrs. Hudson is going to say when she finds out you have given Wiggins one of her napkins, I hate to think," I said dryly.

"It is quite all right, Doctor Watson," that good lady said from the doorway, where she stood with another plate of biscuits. "I buy cheap napery for just that purpose." Mrs. Hudson placed the plate on the table and looked at Holmes. "Just be aware that I am adding the cost to your rent!"

We settled back down with a fresh cup of tea and biscuits. Lestrade selected a ginger biscuit from the plate and turned to Holmes. "When we arrived, you said that we have things to discuss."

"We do indeed, Lestrade."

I thought of something, "When we were at Barrett's, you told him we had come to warn him."

"I did," Holmes affirmed. "I believe he is to be the next victim."

"But why Barrett in particular?" Lestrade asked. "There were others at the party."

"There were, but there are only two of them left that had any connection to the actual excavation of the tomb that resulted in the desecration of the mummy."

I thought for a moment. "You mean Barrett and Lord Ashmoore himself?"

Holmes nodded. "Lord Clavering, Lord Harkness, Granger, the actor Blanding, Lord Ashmoore's cousin – none of them had anything to do with the excavation or the actual unwrapping."

Lestrade frowned. "Doctor Simpson and his two assistants, Cartwright and Evans, unwrapped the mummy."

"Correct."

"Joseph Brown was Barrett's assistant in Egypt," Lestrade continued.

"And no doubt assisted in the theft," I added.

"Robert Wilson provided most of the money for the expedition," said Lestrade.

"Which leaves only Bernard Barrett and Lord Ashmoore himself," said Holmes.

I frowned. "But the curse has more than two more threats to it, does it not?"

"It does, my good Watson, but only the vulture and the devouring of the heart are actually possible to replicate."

Lestrade suddenly intoned: 'May the Blessed Lady Ma'at judge his soul; May Nehebkau cause his Ka and Ba to separate.'" He pulled a sour face. "You are correct, Holmes, those are not events that can be replicated."

"But why Barrett and not Lord Ashmoore as the next victim?" I asked, still puzzled by my friend's logic.

"Think Watson! If Lord Ashmoore is killed, the full weight of the scrutiny of Scotland Yard will descend upon the household. Not to mention Lady Veronica having to go into mourning. Under those circumstances she would be unable to leave the house easily to do anything, let alone commit murder." Holmes broke off to take a sip of his tea. "No, Barrett will be next. With Barrett dead she can bide her time, kill Ashmoore and then make her escape."

"The Irregulars are not really there to protect Lady Ashmoore, are they?" I asked.

"Of course not," Holmes said. "They are there to let us know when the lady makes her move. She and her servants."

"The servants are involved?" I asked.

Holmes nodded.

Lestrade frowned. "All three of them appeared to be Egyptian."

"Exactly, Lestrade," said Holmes. "As such they are most likely to share the lady's beliefs and ideals." He paused. "In fact, I can almost guarantee it."

"What do you mean?" I asked.

Holmes shook his head. "Later, Watson. I will tell you when this is all over."

"Do you think that will be soon?" Lestrade asked.

"Yes. I believe a move against Barrett will be made within the next few days."

Lestrade nodded. "Then, with your permission, I will stick close to Baker Street. Time is likely to be of an essence, so rather than send one of your lads to the Yard, it would be best if I am close by."

Holmes nodded. "They are unlikely to make a move during the daytime. Make sure you are here every day just before sunset."

Lestrade nodded.

We heard a knock on the door downstairs, followed by a murmur of voices, then Mrs. Hudson came in carrying an envelope. "A man just delivered this for you, Mr. Holmes."

Holmes got to his feet and took the envelope from her. "Thank you, Mrs. Hudson."

Mrs. Hudson swiftly cleared the table of all empty plates

and cups before taking her leave.

Holmes opened the envelope and scanned its contents eagerly.

"Who is it from?" I asked.

"Dr. Bond," Holmes replied. "He has heard from his friend in the British Museum's natural history department." He fell silent.

"Well?" I asked, after a minute or so.

"Both venom sacs of the cobra had been removed. Dr. Bond goes on to say that Robert Wilson died from being injected with cobra venom. He also says that he cannot tell how much venom was used to kill Wilson, due to a number of factors, including lack of knowledge as to precisely when the venom was injected. But the death is most definitely murder."

"We already knew that," I observed.

"True, Watson. But Dr. Bond is in a position to positively state that in a court of law. Something that we are not qualified to do."

Lestrade caught on more quickly than I did. "So, Lady Veronica may still have more cobra venom?"

"She may."

"She might use that to kill Barrett!"

"Unlikely, Lestrade. The idea of that killing is to feed the man's liver to a vulture. I do not think she would risk poisoning the bird."

I felt sick. "Do not tell me she tends to feed the bird his liver while the poor man is still alive?"

Holmes fell silent, obviously mulling over my suggestion. He shook his head. "I do not think so, my friend. Islington is a crowded place. Someone would hear his screams. Islington, whilst no longer an upper-class area, is not like Whitechapel where screams would be ignored. People would hear, and people would call the police. That does not suit Lady Veronica's purpose. No, they intend Barrett to be dead when the vulture feeds. But I have no doubt that they will taunt him first."

"Taunt him?" I asked.

"It serves no purpose to kill the man when he does not know why he is going to die. I am sure Barrett will be most thoroughly appraised of his shortcomings before they kill him." Holmes paused. "Attempt to kill him, rather," he amended. "I have hopes that we will prevent that."

Chapter Fifteen

It was slightly after lunch the next day when Cynthia Taverner, Dorothy Watts, and Abasi Tarek visited our rooms.

The ladies took the couch, and Tarek one of dining chairs.

"I trust the meeting was productive?" Holmes said as he seated himself.

"Indeed, it was, Mr. Holmes," Miss Taverner said. "Lady Veronica is most definitely Veronique Meylan."

I looked at Tarek. "You were able to get close enough to identify her?"

"I was, Doctor Watson," Tarek replied. "I escorted the ladies into the house."

"How on Earth did you manage that?" asked Holmes. "You were supposed to be posing as a servant. Servants do not enter the front door of such homes as that of the Ashmoores."

"It was Freddie's idea," Cynthia admitted, referring to her cousin, the somewhat scapegrace Member of Parliament, Frederick Taverner. "He pointed out that since we were supposed to be spending large amounts of time in the East End, any man worth his salt would insist on his womenfolk being accompanied by a footman."

"Your cousin should know," Holmes said dryly. "He spends enough time in the East End."

"He calls it 'researching the conditions of the poor,'"

Cynthia said, with a slight twinkle in her eye.

"That is certainly one description for it," Holmes replied.

To be fair to Freddie Taverner, the man was notorious for spending time in Whitechapel and Wapping. He was known to frequent the various pubs and drinking dens but refused to avail himself of the services of the poor unfortunates reduced to selling themselves in the streets. He considered that to be adding to the problem. The man did, however, distribute money and food to the women. He was a familiar sight on the streets and was known, with some affection, as "Flash Freddie."

"Lady Ashmoore was coming down the stairs as the butler opened the door, so Mr. Tarek managed to get a good look at her."

"I did," Tarek agreed. "The lady is most definitely Veronique Meylan. Much more expensively dressed, of course, but unmistakeable."

"We stayed for a while, naturally, it would have been suspicious to turn around and leave immediately upon arrival," Dorothy added. "Lady Veronica seemed to be most interested in the East End Mission for the Children of Poor Immigrant Workers. She promised a substantial donation."

"How substantial?" I asked.

"She promised £100," Dorothy replied. "That is a vast sum and would provide much relief. It is a great pity that the Mission will never receive it."

"Agreed," Cynthia said. "Freddie was quite taken aback

at the amount promised. He thought it may have been because the lady is not familiar with British currency."

"You talked to your cousin about this?" Holmes asked, eyebrows raised.

Miss Taverner laughed softly. "I really did not have much choice. Freddie was our coachman." She grinned a faintly urchin-like grin. "When Freddie heard why I wanted to borrow his coach, he insisted on driving it himself. Freddie really does love a bit of excitement and helping the great Sherlock Holmes on a case is very much his idea of fun."

My friend sighed. "He was not recognized?"

Cynthia shook her head. "Of course not. He was not dressed in his usual clothes. You know as well as I do, Mr. Holmes, that no one ever looks closely at a servant. Freddie has always loved to drive. The family coachman taught him when he was quite young. I believe my uncle thought it would keep him out of mischief."

"I do not believe that it worked," Holmes replied blandly.

"Of course not. Freddie and mischief go together like cats and cream." Miss Taverner shook her head again. "It is sometimes hard to reconcile my cousin's personality with the fact he is a Member of Parliament."

"I believe it is his personal charm, Cynthia," Dorothy said with a slight smile. "He is gracious, and pleasant, with a boyish enthusiasm for life. People cannot help but like him and want to help him."

"A useful fact to know," Holmes commented, "but not germane to the case."

Dorothy nodded and got to her feet. "We have completed our task." She paused. "Unless you have anything else that you wish us to do?"

Holmes shook his head. "I think not. You have all done remarkable well with what was required."

The ladies and Tarek went to take their leave. A thought struck me. "Holmes," I said.

"What is it, Watson?"

"Should there not be a lady present when we arrest Lady Veronica? There may be unpleasantness otherwise."

My friend thought for a moment. "A good thought, my friend. We do not want accusations of brutality bandied about. We do need to remember that the lady is married to an aristocrat with connections."

Cynthia and Dorothy exchanged a look. "We will both come," Cynthia said.

"We will not take part in the arrest," Dorothy added. "But we will be there to handle Lady Veronica. You both know what I am capable of, and I am sure that Cynthia is equally capable. So, there is no need to worry about our safety."

"Lestrade may not be happy having you present," Holmes warned.

Dorothy smiled. "I shall clear it with your brother. This is a matter involving a foreign government, to some extent, and as such there should be a representative of our government present."

"That will certainly pin down any objections that Lestrade may make," Holmes said, with some amusement. "You are learning a great deal from my brother."

"He is an excellent teacher on the subject of practical politics," Dorothy replied.

Cynthia then said, "I have no doubt that Freddie will wish to accompany us. No doubt driving his own coach again." She smiled at my friend before he could object. "Besides which, it would be a little crowded with the five of us in one coach."

"Do you wish to attend, Mr. Tarek?" I asked.

The man shook his head. "No, thank you, Doctor Watson. I fear it would be a great deal more excitement than I care for. I trust that you and Mr. Holmes, and the good Inspector Lestrade, will see this through to a satisfactory conclusion."

"Very well," Holmes said. "Ladies do be here around sunset each day. It is unlikely that anything will happen before nightfall."

Cynthia nodded. "It is hard to cover nefarious activities during daylight hours. The night covers all sins, as the saying goes."

"Indeed," Holmes replied.

Abasi Tarek escorted the ladies from the room, with a slight bow to us.

Chapter Sixteen

As Holmes had warned, Lestrade did not take well to the idea of Miss Taverner and Miss Watts accompanying us. Even though Lestrade himself had seen Dorothy save my life, he still viewed her with the utmost chivalry. As, indeed, he did most women. But by the time the ladies arrived, he had reconciled himself to the idea. "It isn't as though I have any choice, is it?" he commented dryly.

We both agreed with him that this was indeed the case.

Both ladies wore rational dresses that allowed them more freedom of movement than traditional gowns allowed. The Rational Dress Society had started in 1881, with the idea of specially designed gowns that reduced weight, and the necessity of corsets, allowing women to undertake more athletic pursuits, such as bicycle riding. The popular garment, the divided skirt, which both Cynthia and Dorothy were wearing, had been invented by Viscountess Florence Wallace Pomeroy, Lady Haberton.

Freddie Taverner was not with them. Cynthia saw my confusion and guessed its source. "Freddie is driving the coach, again. He has therefore remained downstairs. I believe he is talking with Inspector Lestrade's constables about their working conditions."

Lestrade stifled a groan.

It was not until late the next afternoon that a note was received from Jamrach's Animal Emporium advising us that the vulture had arrived and had been delivered to the house in

Islington.

That very night brought two breathless members of the Baker Street Irregulars to our rooms.

"Wiggins sent me, Mr. 'Olmes," the first lad gasped out. "'E said ter tell yer that the toffy lady's carriage 'as left the 'ouse, but wivout the lady in it. Wiggins finks they've gone ter git the cove what grubs in the dirt."

The second lad, who, when they opened their mouth, I realized was a girl, nodded. "Liz is right. A posh carriage rolled up an' two blokes got out an' went into the dirt grubber's flat. Weren't in there long. The bloke came out wiv them an' they got in the coach an' drove orf."

"Well done," Holmes said. He dug into his pocket for some coins. "Here is a small thank you. See Wiggins later for your full pay, Lizard and...?"

"I be Jenny, Mr. 'Olmes."

"...and Jenny. Again, well done."

The Irregulars beamed at him, their coins clutched tightly in their fists, before turning and rushing out of the door.

Holmes turned to us. "Come now, everyone, the game is afoot. Watson, you have your pistol?"

I patted my coat pocket. "Put it in my coat this afternoon. I thought we might need it."

"Stout fellow!"

We all hastened downstairs to where the police growler

and Freddie Taverner's coach waited by the kerb.

I saw with some amusement that Frederick Taverner, M.P., was wearing a well maintained, but definitely old, ulster coat with a well-brushed, but also equally aged, low crown top hat. The ulster was similar to the Inverness, which Holmes favoured for country excursions. The difference being that the ulster had a short cape that only came down to the elbows, allowing the freedom of movement that a coachman needed. Like the Inverness the ulster was usually made of a hard-wearing material such as herringbone or tweed.

In short, Freddie Taverner looked like the perfectly respectable coachman of some middle-class, but prosperous, businessman. He went to step down from the coach, but Holmes shook his head. Holmes himself handed Cynthia and Dorothy into the coach.

"Thankee kindly, sir," Taverner said in a soft drawl.

Holmes looked up at him with slight asperity. "Do not overdo it, Taverner." Then he turned away to join Lestrade in the growler. Freddie Taverner gave me a wink as I went to join Holmes.

As the growler pulled away from the kerb, Holmes commented, "If he were not a Member of Parliament, Freddie Taverner would have made a passible thespian, but for the fact he has a tendency to somewhat over-egg the pudding."

I chuckled. "His accent was that bad?"

"Not entirely, he could pass for a man from the streets

who has had some education. But it would be too easy for his station to be given away by an injudicious word. Much better to remain silent and simply nod the head. Most coachmen are taciturn by nature anyway."

"Preferring the company of their horses to that of their fellow men?" Lestrade asked with some amusement.

"As you say, Lestrade," Holmes replied. With that Holmes sank back in his seat and refused to converse anymore.

The trip to Islington was, thankfully, a short one. We were all on edge. I at least, was praying that we would arrive in time to save Barrett from a ghastly death.

Lestrade's inner turmoil was displayed by the twitching of his moustache. Only Holmes sat quietly; no movement or expression gave away his thoughts as he gazed out of the window.

We parked both carriages slightly down the street from the Ashmoore house. The carriage we had seen at Ashmoore's Chiswick house stood in the street in front of the house.

Wiggins slid out of the darkness as we left the coach.

"The bird was delivered yesterdee, Mr. 'Olmes. Bloody ugly thing it is." He spotted Cynthia and Dorothy exiting their coach. "'Eck. Didn't know there was ladies comin'. 'Pologies, ladies."

"That is quite all right, Wiggins," Dorothy said with a smile. "I am sure that we have both heard worse."

Wiggins leaned forward to look at her and grinned. "'Tis

Miss Dorothy, ain't it? You was involved in that rum do wiv Archie in the Strand?"

"I was."

Wiggins sketched a little bow. "We wasn't introduced that day. But I'm guessin' Mr. 'Olmes told yer me name. Pleased ter meet ya, Miss Dorothy. I'm Wiggins."

Wiggins had been active in the case that I called *The Molly-Boy Murders* where we had first met Dorothy and had been present at a confrontation with a police constable that had resulted in the constable receiving a broken nose. Archie was a former Irregular who had been adopted by a police sergeant.

Wiggins looked at Miss Taverner. Dorothy introduced them. "Wiggins, this is Miss Cynthia Taverner. Cynthia, this is Wiggins."

Wiggins' look turned speculative. "Yer the lady dick what's related to Flash Freddie?"

Cynthia was struggling to keep her face straight. "I am."

"Mebbe we should talk later. Me an' the lads could do fer you what we does for Mr. 'Olmes. Same rates."

Holmes raised his eyebrows. "Leaving me, Wiggins?"

"Never, Mr. 'Olmes. But you don't always 'ave jobs fer us. We're good at what we does. An' I reckon if the lady dick is workin' wiv you, then you reckon she's pretty good. We only works fer the best, after all."

There was a muffled snort of laughter from the top of

Taverner's coach. Wiggins turned to look. His eyes went wide. "Cor! Tis Flash Freddie 'isself!"

Freddie Taverner doffed his topper to Wiggins, with a broad grin.

Wiggins turned back to Holmes. "Anyway, the bird was delivered yesterdee. The servants brought the dirt grubber back just 'fore yer arrived."

"We had best hurry, Holmes," I said. Before they kill him."

Wiggins shook his head. "Don't worry, Doc, they ain't goin' to do that fer a bit."

"What makes you say that?" Lestrade asked.

"They dragged 'im out of the coach. 'Is 'ead was sort of lollin' from side ter side. Pretty clear they'd coshed 'im one. They'll wait till 'e's come round 'fore they off 'im. Stands ter reason. If they'd just wanted 'im dead, they'd killed 'im at 'is flat. No need to drag 'im out 'ere."

"Well-reasoned, Wiggins," Holmes said with a smile. "We will make a detective out of you yet."

The lad grinned at the praise. A small shadow detached itself from beside the house and slid up to us. It was another of the Irregulars. "I thinks they're gunna start on the cove," the lad told Wiggins. "One o' the blokes chucked water on 'im and 'e sorta spluttered awake. They was tyin' 'im down when I came ter get yer."

"Righto, Tom, Mr. 'Olmes and 'is pals will take care o'

169

it. Won't yer, Mr. 'Olmes?"

"We will, Wiggins. Someone needs to show us exactly where to go."

Tom beckoned to us. "This way, gents."

Holme and I, with Lestrade and two of the accompanying police constables, followed the lad down the alley beside the house.

Cynthia and Dorothy returned to Taverner's coach to wait. Their part would come when Lady Veronica was arrested.

As we approached the small carriage-house, we could hear voices. A furtive glance through the one small window showed Bernard Barrett, a bruise beginning to form on what could be seen of the left side of his face, tied down on what appeared to be an old bed frame. His upper clothing had been cut from him and hung in rags from his wrists. Some of the cloth had been used to gag him. A bulging in Barrett's cheeks spoke of cloth wadded into his mouth, then a strip of cloth tied around his head.

Masuda and Waaiz stood one at each end of the bed frame. One of them held a butcher's knife in his hands, twisting it to and fro; allowing the light from the lantern suspended over head to play over the blade. The act was clearly designed to terrify their captive, as Barrett could barely take his eyes from the glistening steel. He only did so to cast despairing looks to where an evil looking bird sat on a perch.

"*Neophron percnopterus*," Holmes murmured in my ear.

"One of the world's smaller vultures, but still impressive, yes?"

It was, I thought, impressively ugly. The bird was about the size of a small chicken, with a bright yellow beak that ended with a cruel hook. Its feathers were a dull white with black feathers visible in the wings. The oddest feature was the neck. Where a strange arrangement of feathers gave the bird the appearance of having a mane, resulting in it looking vaguely like some odd, avian, lion.

A small door set into the larger door of the carriage house opened, and Lady Veronica swept in. I shuddered in revulsion at the cold, cruel, look on her face. A look that almost exactly matched that of the vulture. She gave the bound man a look of sheer loathing. "Bernard Barrett, you are guilty of the violation of the tomb and the eternal resting place of Neb-Heka-Ra, and as such you shall suffer under the beak and talons of Nekhbet." She took a deep breath and began to intone "I am Neb-Heka-Ra, First among Magicians…"

"Now!" Holmes roared.

The three of us, followed by the two constables rushed in through the small door.

All three killers looked at us in momentary shock, before Lady Veronica screamed in outrage. The one holding the knife flew at Holmes, knife raised. My pistol was in my hand, and I did not hesitate, shooting the man in the shoulder. He spun around, dropping the knife to the ground in his agony.

One of the constables pounced on him, ignoring his cries of pain, and handcuffed him. Holmes and the other constable brought the second man to the ground.

I heard Lestrade cry out in pain and then swear. I spun around, to see him standing there with his hand clasped to his face; blood staining his cheek.

"I tried to grab her. The witch slashed me with her nails."

"Let me look," I said.

Lestrade removed his hand from his face. I examined him closely. "Surface only, thank goodness. But we need to get them cleaned, otherwise infection is a possibility. Human fingernails are less than clean."

Cynthia spoke from the doorway. "Freddie usually carries brandy or whisky with him. That should clean the inspector's wounds, at least for now."

Holmes looked around from where they had managed to handcuff the second man.

"I know," Cynthia said, "We were to stay with the coaches. However, I came to let you know that the bird has flown. Lady Veronica can obviously drive as she came racing out, got on the coach and drove it away. I am afraid that Dorothy and I were too far away to react."

Holmes shrugged. "It does not matter. There is only one place she could go."

"Chiswick?" Lestrade asked.

"Chiswick," Holmes agreed.

Holmes then turned to where Barrett was slumped in his bonds.

I removed the gag as Lestrade cut him free from the ropes.

Cynthia had returned to Freddie's carriage and then returned with Freddie, Dorothy, and a flask of whisky. Freddie took one look at Barrett and poured out a nip of the spirit for the man. Barrett drank it gratefully.

"I should have listened to you," he said in a hoarse whisper.

"What on Earth possessed you to go with them? Especially after our warning," Lestrade said, wincing as I washed his wounds with the whisky..

Barrett closed his eyes. "They said they came from Lord Ashmoore. That he wanted to speak to me urgently about another excavation. As I went to get into the carriage, one of them hit me in the head. The next thing I knew I was waking up here. In this deplorable state."

It was then that I noticed that Dorothy had a horse blanket draped over her arm. She handed it to me and inclined her head towards Barrett. I carefully wrapped the now shaking man in the blanket.

"Holmes," I said. "I do not want to leave Barrett alone. He is suffering from shock."

"If you like, Doctor Watson," Freddie Taverner said. "I shall take Barrett home with me. My footmen will keep an eye on him, and he will know that he is safe."

"Thank you, Mr. Taverner," Holmes said. "That is an excellent solution.

I nodded my agreement. "Make sure Barrett is kept warm and quiet. Also hot, sweet, tea will help."

Taverner nodded. "Between us, I am sure my servants and I can find fresh clothes for him as well. We will keep him safe until Inspector Lestrade or another officer can take his statement."

I looked around to see that Cynthia had slipped away. I spotted her outside with her arm around a woman who was weeping bitterly. She led the woman towards us.

"This is Dina. The wife of Masuda," Cynthia explained softly. "She is most distressed by what has happened."

Lestrade frowned. "I should arrest her as well."

The woman, Dina, let out a wail. Cynthia soothed her and glared at Lestrade. "I do not think that is necessary, inspector."

"Now look here, Miss…"

"Cynthia is correct, Lestrade," Dorothy said softly. "A wife is not responsible for the actions of her husband. Our laws clearly state that, as you well know. Besides, Cynthia and I will remain here with her until a statement can be taken."

Lestrade sighed and then grumbled, "Oh, very well. I shall send someone along in the morning." He paused. "What if Lady Veronica comes back?"

Dorothy patted her reticule. "I have my trusty derringer in here, Lestrade. And I am an excellent shot."

"That would certainly save us a lot of trouble," Lestrade said.

"And no doubt cause a great many more problems," Holmes said sharply. "Come, gentlemen, we must be on our way to Chiswick."

Chapter Seventeen

The Ashmoore household was in an uproar when we arrived. The butler, looking more harassed than a man in his position is wont, let us in. When we asked for Lord Ashmoore, he simply pointed up the stairs to where most of the noise seemed to be coming from.

We headed upstairs, passing clusters of servants in their night attire, huddled together as if for warmth like so many startled chickens. At length we came across Lord Ashmoore, himself in his night clothes, begging frantically outside a door that was obviously locked. He turned to us as we approached.

Lord Ashmoore's countenance was wild with fear. "My wife arrived back alone, driving the coach. She would not say what happened to her servants. Then she almost flew up the stairs and has locked herself in her room."

"We know what has happened, Lord Ashmoore," Lestrade said. "We need to speak with your wife urgently." He then proceeded to hammer on the door. "Please open up, Lady Ashmoore, it is the police."

"You are wasting your time, Lestrade," Holmes said softly. My friend looked around until he spotted several of the lurking footmen. "You! Break this door down."

The men looked at Lord Ashmoore. His Lordship gave a hesitant nod. The men then hurried away, returning with both a sledgehammer and a mattock. As they hurried up the stairs, Holmes placed his hand on Lord Ashmoore's arm. "You must prepare yourself for a great shock, Lord Ashmoore," Holmes gently murmured.

Ashmoore's face drained of all colour and for a moment I thought he would pass out. I signalled to the butler to bring His Lordship a glass of brandy. Whatever waited behind that door, I was sure that the man was going to have need of it.

The footmen made short work of the door. Lestrade entered first and stopped dead in the doorway. I looked over his shoulder.

Lady Veronica lay upon her bed. Her face set in the grim rictus of death.

I pushed my way into the room and hurried to her bedside. As I got closer, I could see a ribbon tied around her left arm in a tourniquet. Upon the bed lay a syringe that had clearly fallen from her arm in her death throes.

"We will need to send for Doctor Bond," Holmes said quietly. "But I can tell you now that the cause of death was the injection of the venom of *Naja haje* directly into the vein of the left arm."

"Egyptian cobra venom?" I asked. "But…"

"Need I remind you that the cobra has *two* venom sacs?"

Lestrade closed his eyes. "Both sacs were missing from the dead cobra we found."

"Exactly," Holmes said softly.

"She must have planned this. For if things went wrong," Lestrade said.

Holmes nodded silently.

Lord Ashmoore had collapsed beside the bed, his eyes wide in shock. I stepped up. Placing my hand on his shoulder to provide what little comfort I could. As I did so, I noticed an envelope upon the pillow. I reached across and picked it up.

"Holmes, this is addressed to you."

My friend took it from my hand. Lord Ashmoore looked up. "My wife kills herself and leaves a note for you?" His tone held both grief and disbelief.

Holmes looked around. Many of the servants were clustered around the door, peeping into the room.

"I think we need to continue this somewhere a little more private."

Lestrade and I helped the stricken Lord Ashmoore to his feet and escorted him to his study. The butler followed, bringing the requested brandy for Lord Ashmoore.

Once we were seated Holmes asked, "Before I read the letter, Lord Ashmoore, I must ask, how well did you know your wife before you married her?"

Ashmoore took a sip of his brandy. "Not well at all," he finally admitted. "She was the daughter of Thierry Meylan, the man who arranged to get the mummy of Neb-Heka-Ra and his grave goods out of Egypt. He died in Naples. The poor girl was distraught and alone. I could not, in good conscience leave her alone, attended only by three servants, in a foreign city. I proposed marriage, and she accepted. I will admit, gentlemen, that I was very taken by her looks and charming manners. I was in need of another wife, so it was an easy decision to make. Veronica is..." Lord Ashmoore paused for a second, swallowed hard and then continued, "...was...easy to love."

Holmes nodded then looked down at the letter in his hands. Getting to his feet he picked up a letter opener from the top of the desk and carefully slit the envelope. He read the contents in silence. Lestrade and I were almost breathless with anticipation. Lord Ashmoore had, understandably, sunk into melancholy misery.

It was Lestrade who asked: "What does it say?"

Holmes looked up at us for a long moment. Then sighed, cleared his throat, and read aloud, "Dear Mr. Holmes. I had hoped not to be writing this letter. If I have done so it is because you have won. Before I was Lady Veronica Ashmoore, I was Veronique Meylan, daughter of Thierry Meylan and an Egyptian woman named Aya..."

Lord Ashmoore looked up. "Meylan told me his wife was Italian."

"That may well have been the case, Lord Ashmoore," Holmes replied. "But we have it on very good authority that your wife was the daughter of his mistress."

Lord Ashmoore looked horrified. I could see whence his horror arose, as much as I deplored it. For a man of his position marrying a lower-class woman was one thing, but to marry a bastard, even one acknowledged by her father, was just not acceptable. Never mind that half the aristocracy were merrily producing bastards at a speed that many a modern factory would envy. Hypocrisy was an enduring hallmark of Britain's upper classes.

Holmes went back to the letter. "My mother was descended from Neb-Heka-Ra. Our family has guarded his last resting place since the day he was entombed."

"Impossible," Lestrade snorted.

Holmes looked up from the letter. "Improbable, Lestrade, yes. Impossible, not necessarily so. After all, our dear queen reckons her ancestry back to the Norse god Odin or Wotan."

Lestrade blinked. "She does?"

"According to the writings of Icelandic politician and historian Snorri Sturluson, she is so descended. If I may continue?" Holmes tone was a trifle testy.

Lestrade nodded.

Holmes continued to read: "We kept his tomb safe until Ashmoore and Barrett came along. Both with their grotesque desires to rip Egypt's treasures from her bosom. My father knew of the existence of my ancestor's tomb, and, for love of my mother forbore from trespassing. Then my mother died, and my father's greed came to mean more to him than anything else. Even my happiness. So, when he ignored my pleas and conspired to loot the tomb of Neb-Heka-Ra, I knew he had to be punished, along with those that encouraged him in the act. In deference to the fact that he was my father, I did not exact the full penalty, and simply gave him arsenic."

"Some deference," Lestrade muttered. I nodded my agreement.

Holmes glared at Lestrade and continued. "The fool of a doctor in Naples simply wrote the death off as typhoid or typhus. Or perhaps cholera. I did not take much notice. It matters not which one it was. It mattered only that he was dead. It seemed like a gift from the gods when Ashmoore offered to marry me. I agreed immediately as there was truly no other way that I could get close enough to take vengeance on those responsible for the desecration. The mummy unwrapping party was the vilest of abominations. I do wonder if my dear husband would have liked to see the body of one of his illustrious ancestors mauled about so."

I noted that Lord Ashmoore looked startled, and then vaguely ashamed, as if such a thought had not occurred to him before. Likely it had not.

Holmes went on, "The party gave me a chance to discover names, and my husband's secretary kept such careful notes that it was easy to find the addresses of those I considered most at fault. My husband, of course, Barrett, the banker, the doctor and his two assistants. I had no intention of harming anyone else who attended the party. They were simply invited guests, who had not been involved in the actual desecration. It was sheer good luck that Lord Clavering had a crocodile. Or perhaps not. I thought that Ma'at was assisting us as so many things fell so easily into place. Until you appeared, Mr. Holmes. It then became clear that the justice of this country is not like Ma'at of my homeland. That your Lady of Justice and Order did not like what we were doing. That is when I sat down to write this letter. I do not know if my cousins, Masuda and Waaiz…"

"Cousins?" I exclaimed. "I thought they were servants!"

"Oh, they are definitely related, Watson," Holmes said. "I realised that quite early on." He turned back to the letter. "…my cousins, Masuda and Waaiz were both willing assistants in the task. It was Masuda who found Barrett's assistant, the man Brown, for me, as he was not invited to the party. I beg mercy, however for Masuda's wife Dina. She knows nothing of these events. Moreover, she is carrying Masuda's first, and now no doubt only, child."

"I am sure we can ensure that the lady is well attended to. Perhaps Mr Tarek could assist?" Lestrade said.

"Excellent idea, Lestrade," I said.

Holmes folded up the letter. "That is it. The letter is simply signed 'Veronique Meylan.'"

Lord Ashmoore was sitting in his chair, his face ashen.

Holmes looked at him. "You can think yourself lucky, Lord Ashmoore."

"Lucky? How in God's name do you work that out?"

"There was one more death mentioned in the curse. That would have been your fate. To have the very heart carved out of you."

"How would she…?" Lord Ashmoore's voice trailed off.

"I suspect a message would have been sent begging you to come to the Islington house. There you would have been killed and the others escaped to Egypt. They would have been well away before the alarm could have been raised."

Lord Ashmoore sank his head into his hands. I went to the door and signalled the butler to take the man up to bed. Lestrade went to organize the police response, and the police growler dropped us back at Baker Street before heading on to Scotland Yard.

Chapter Eighteen

We were almost immediately immersed in another case, and it was almost three months later that I saw in the newspaper that Masuda and Waaiz had been hanged at Pentonville prison. That very day a note arrived from Mycroft inviting us to the Diogenes Club that evening.

It was no surprise to find Lestrade present, but somewhat of one to find both Henry Cavanagh and Abasi Tarek present. Freddie Taverner arrived shortly after we did.

Mycroft poured everyone, apart from Tarek, a brandy. Tarek was offered coffee, which he accepted with pleasure. "It is rare, indeed, Mr. Holmes, to find an Englishman who understands that a man of my faith does not drink alcohol."

"You will find, Mr. Tarek," Holmes said, "That there is very little that my brother does not know."

"Except, perhaps, how you knew that Masuda and Waaiz were cousins of Lady Veronica," I said. I had not forgotten Holmes's comment when reading the lady's last letter. "I am sure even Mycroft could not have known that."

"It was Mr. Cavanagh here that pointed me in that direction," Holmes said.

The man in question looked startled. "I did?"

"When you showed me the mummy of Neb-Heka-Ra. The corpse had quite distinctive ears. Lady Veronica, as well as Masuda and Waaiz, had exactly the same ears."

"But how did you know there were cousins?" Taverner

asked.

"The kinship was not exact. I knew they had to be close family, but not brothers. If they had been brothers, then Thierry Meylan would have no doubt pushed them forward in his business."

"You are correct, Mr. Holmes," Tarek said. "Masuda and Waaiz were the sons of Veronique's mother's youngest brother."

"I was at the execution this morning," Lestrade said sombrely. "Neither of the men had anything of note to say. They both went to the gallows as proud as Lucifer himself."

"Did they confess?" I asked curiously.

"According to the governor of the prison Masuda had confirmed all that happened, and they did not fear death. The only thing that held concern for them was the theft of the bone saw."

"What?" I blinked in astonishment.

"The theft of the bone saw was weighing more heavily on their minds than the fact they had murdered five men and attempted to murder a sixth." Lestrade shook his head at the very idea.

"What did happen to the bone saw?" I asked.

"Apparently, they chucked it in the Thames when they left Clavering's manor. It's probably several feet deep in mud by now."

"What has happened to Lord Ashmoore?" Tarek asked.

"His Lordship has left London," Mycroft replied. "He felt unable to face the intense scrutiny that he would no doubt have been under. He has closed his Chiswick house, and his Islington one, and gone to the Continent. To Portugal, I believe."

"Why there?" I asked.

"Possibly because he is unlikely to run into anyone he knows," Holmes said, "Unlike if he went to France, or Italy, or even Germany."

Mycroft nodded. "As you say, Sherlock. Dorothy mentioned to me the donation that Lady Veronica had promised to the East End Mission for the Children of Immigrant Workers. Before Lord Ashmoore left our shores, he was prevailed upon to donate the promised amount of £100."

"Dorothy will be pleased to hear that," I said.

"I do like to keep my staff happy, Doctor Watson." Mycroft turned to Freddie Taverner, "Speaking of staff, I was very much impressed by your cousin."

"I trust you are not thinking of trying to recruit her," Taverner said with a smile. "Cynthia has her own business and would not be amenable to closing it down, even to work for the government."

"I was thinking more along the lines of engaging her for special cases, much as I do my brother. I believe that she got on well with Miss Watt."

"She did," I observed. "They were friends within minutes of meeting."

Mycroft gave a self-satisfied smile at my comment. It was obvious to us all that he already had plans for Miss Taverner.

"Before Lord Ashmoore left," Cavanagh said, getting the conversation back on track, "he gave all of his Egyptian artifacts to the British Museum. Including the contents of the tomb of Neb-Heka-Ra. He appears to have quite lost his taste for Egyptian antiquities."

"If I might make a suggestion," Holmes said, "…it would be a move of good faith to return such items to Egypt."

Cavanagh nodded. He looked across at Abasi Tarek. "You are the Khedive's agent, I believe?"

"I am, Mr. Cavanagh."

"Then come tomorrow morning to my office at the British Museum and we shall arrange for the formal return of all items."

"Thank you, Mr. Cavanagh, on behalf of both myself and the Khedive." Abasi Tarek looked around at us. "Inspector Lestrade mentioned the widow of Masuda to me. It seems the lady has been left in quite dire conditions. I have arranged for the lady to marry an Egyptian merchant here in London. He is an old man, without children, he was happy to take on a pregnant wife. He has promised that he will raise the child as his own. He is a good man and will treat her well. I have

187

known him for quite a few years. He will keep his word."

"What of Lady Veronica's corpse?" I asked. "I saw no funeral mentioned in the newspapers."

"Lord Ashmoore, declined to allow his wife to be interred in the family tomb," Mycroft said. "She has been buried discreetly in an unmarked grave. Mr Tarek kindly assisted with the appropriate rites."

"That really only leaves Barrett," Taverner observed.

"Mr. Barrett has also been taken care of," Mycroft said. "He is persona non grata in Egypt, and rightfully so."

Cavanagh sighed. "He is a good archaeologist. It is a pity his skills will go to waste."

"They will not go to waste," Mycroft assured Cavanagh with a slight smile. "Mr. Barrett has already left London to join an expedition in Mesopotamia. A Mr. Nigel Withers is accompanying him as his new secretary."

We all got to our feet to leave, when Taverner exclaimed, "What about the vulture?"

"I assume that it was returned to Jamrach's Animal Emporium," I said.

Mycroft shook his head. "I believe Lord Clavering has given the bird a home."

"I wonder what he will name it?" Lestrade mused. "He has a tiger named Priscilla, and a crocodile named Sobek."

Mycroft's lips twitched slightly. "I understand,

Inspector, that His Lordship intends to name the bird Sherlock."

"An interesting name for an interesting bird," my friend said dryly. "Come, Watson, I think a little supper at Simpson's is called for."

Author's Notes

The Valley of the Magicians exists only in my imagination. As far as I am aware no equivalent of the Valley of the Kings for the various priesthoods has been discovered. But who knows what lies buried beneath the streets of Cairo?

A few people might wonder at Dr. Simpson performing surgeries in people's homes. I did not make that up. It was common practice up until the late 1920s for tonsillectomies to be performed at home using ether dripped through a mesh strainer as anaesthetic.

I have been asked about my descriptions of Victorian mortuaries in my books. I was fortunate to visit the Jack the Ripper Museum in Cable Street in London's East End where there is a reproduction of a Victorian mortuary in the basement. The room has corpse drawers from the local mortuary as well as a genuine wooden post-mortem table that still bears the stains of use. The mortuary in question is where at least one of the Ripper's victims was examined. I have been using that reconstruction as the basis for the mortuary scenes in my books.

The incident with the tiger and the child outside of Jamrach's Animal Emporium actually did happen. There is a statue at Tobacco Dock in Wapping that commemorates the event.

Onto the subject of the language used in the book:

The word "dick" that is used to mean a detective is authentic street cant. It entered the English language around 1864. It was a slang term that meant to watch or to see and eventually morphed into a noun. The word is thought to have derived from the Romany word "dik" meaning to look or to see. Interestingly, it continued to evolve as a verb, becoming "dekko" meaning, again, to look or to see.

The word "flash" which meant to show off, also had the meaning of being something special. Which, you have to admit, Freddie Taverner is exactly that.

Allison Harvey bought a package on Kickstarter for the naming of a character which she gifted to her aunt. This is the sterling housekeeper in the novel, Diana Myers. I do hope Ms. Myers enjoys her appearance.

As per usual, a number of books were consulted in the course of writing. The major ones were:

"A Season in Egypt 1887" by Flinders Petrie;

"The British Museum: The History of Britain's Most Famous Public Museum" – author anonymous but published by Charles Rivers Editors;

"Death and Burial in Ancient Egypt" by Salima Ikram;

"Practical Egyptian Magic" by Murry Hope;

"The Egyptian Book of the Dead" by E. A. Wallis Budge;

"Crocodiles and Alligators" – consulting editor Charles A. Ross, published by Golden Press P/L 1989;

"Beeton's Book of Household Management – Facsimile Edition" – published in 1977.

Books are not written in a vacuum and there are always people to thank. In this case they are:

Dr. Andrea Williams – for her help with French names.

Janelle Atkins – for the loan of the book on Egyptian magic.

Penny Merritt – for finding other books that I desperately needed and for listening when I had written myself into a corner and then suggesting ways to get myself out.

Richard Ryan - who edits my novels;

Brian Belanger - who creates such wonderfully atmospheric covers.

And last, but definitely not least, Steve Emecz, who publishes my books. I will forever be grateful to you, Steve, for taking a punt on me.

Margaret Walsh

Melbourne, August 2022

www.ingramcontent.com/pod-product-compliance
Lightning Source LLC
Chambersburg PA
CBHW070021260626
47159CB00005B/1906